ABOUT THE AUTHOR

Claire Hennessy lives in Knocklyon, Dublin, and is in third year at school. Apart from writing, her hobbies include reading and running up huge phone bills by spending way too much time on the Internet. She's not exactly sporty but likes swimming, hockey and athletics. TV programmes she's addicted to include *Buffy, Angel, Dawson's Creek, Popular, ER* and *Star Trek*. She's a certified chocoholic and also belongs to that strange group of people who actually like maths. According to the personality test at thespark.com, she's an artist. *Being Her Sister* is her second book.

Also by Claire Hennessy
Dear Diary

Being Her Sister

Claire Hennessy

POOLBEG
FOR CHILDREN

Published 2001
by Poolbeg Press Ltd.
123 Baldoyle Industrial Estate
Dublin 13, Ireland
Email: poolbeg@poolbeg.com
www.poolbeg.com

The moral right of the author has been asserted.

1 3 5 7 9 10 8 6 4 2

A catalogue record for this book is available from the British Library.

ISBN 1 84223 017 4

Cover design by Slatter-Anderson
Typeset by Patricia Hope in Goudy 11.5/15

Printed and bound in Great Britain by
The Guernsey Press Co. Ltd, Guernsey, Channel Islands

ACKNOWLEDGEMENTS

Oh God! Here's the hard bit! First of all, thanks to my parents, without whom I wouldn't be here, and you wouldn't be reading this, um, literary masterpiece. (OK, so it's not exactly Shakespeare, but hey! Enjoy!)

Thanks to all at Poolbeg, again without whom you wouldn't be reading this.

Thanks to all my relatives, friends, teachers and so on who have been encouraging and very occasionally helpful. Special thanks to all my friends from CTYI 2000. I love you all! And to those friends who suffer through the days at Beaufort with me, thanks a million. (None of the characters is based on any of you. Don't worry!)

To my brother, Tim –
who knows what it's like to have a sister from hell!

1

Danielle

It's hard not be jealous of Rachel. I mean, if you had a little sister who was nearly two years younger than you and yet better than you at everything, wouldn't you spend most of your time feeling depressed?

I certainly do, anyway. I'm nearly fourteen and in second year at the local community school. She's twelve and she's also in second year. Mum sent her to school when she was barely four as she "showed so much potential", and then the teachers moved her ahead in primary school as she was so smart. She, of course, is too intelligent for the community school. My parents sent her to this posh girls' school three miles away. My mum gets up early to drive her there every morning.

"Danielle," she says to me whenever I complain, "don't you want your sister to get the best education she can?" In response I think, "Don't you want *me* to get the best education I can?" I never actually say it, though. I don't care

1

about getting an education, it's the principle of the thing. It's that they worship Rachel and couldn't be bothered about me.

Rachel, naturally, never gets into trouble. I try not to, but it's hard when every little thing looks like murder next to her immaculate record. And the not-so-little things, too, like when my friends and I said we were going to each other's houses to sleepover when we really went to this disco in town and had a great time there, well, for a while. Then one guy wouldn't leave Tara alone, and another one kept on pushing Liz and Naomi to take drugs, so we left and swore we'd never go back. We got caught and I got grounded for ages. That was last year and I still don't want to go back there. Anyway, the point is that the most trouble Rachel ever gets into is forgetting to do a tiny bit of her homework.

Rachel is also much prettier than me. She has beautiful long chestnut hair and deep green eyes and a flawless complexion. My hair is the same shade as hers, but last summer I got it cut really short and have been regretting it ever since. I hate it now. It's not extremely short any more, it's long enough to tie back into a tiny ponytail, but I still absolutely despise it. One of my friends from school, Mark, says he loves my hair, though. It still doesn't convince me. He's always flirting with me, anyway, so he probably doesn't mean it.

I have hazel eyes, at least that's how Rachel describes them. We both have light little freckles on our noses, and we tend not to get spots that often, particularly her. She never seems to understand that sometimes there are times when you *have* to stuff your face with chocolate.

There are three more weeks until Christmas. We get our holidays on the twentieth, a Tuesday. Our Christmas exams start on the thirteenth, a week before that. No doubt Rachel is going to get all A's. And I will probably get B's or C's if I'm lucky. That's the way it always is. The lowest score I ever got was 35%. The lowest she has ever got was 85%. That really depresses me. I mean, she's younger than me and yet better than me at everything. We went to the same primary school but we were in different classes, and had different friends, so at least we weren't constantly being compared to each other. It's not that I want to be a brain, I don't even care about school, really, but I hate feeling inferior to people. Especially when it's my little sister.

My friends all think she's brilliant, of course, to be twenty months younger than me and still be in the same year as me. My friend Tara is having a slumber party tonight and she's invited both of us. I'm dreading it. I didn't think Rachel would want to go, as she never goes to parties or discos or anything – she must think they're too frivolous or something – but she agreed to come to this one.

I am now tossing things into a black Adidas bag for the slumber party. I have my pyjamas, naturally, with pictures of the cast of *Friends* on the top, and my toothbrush, hairbrush, deodorant, and clothes for tomorrow. I wonder what Rachel will bring. I don't think she's ever gone to a slumber party before, actually.

Tara is having this slumber party for Christmas. You see, she's going to Australia for a month, starting on the 10th, a Saturday, so this is kind of like a goodbye party. I'm incredibly jealous. While we're freezing here, she'll be off lying on beaches and sunbathing. For a month! Tara's family are wealthier than the average. They live in a normal house and everything, but they have four TVs – with every channel – and go on really long holidays in the summer. Tara was supposed to be going to the same posh school Rachel is at, but she begged her parents to let her go to our school.

I can't wait until Christmas, I think. I love it so much. The excited atmosphere that comes with it. The Christmas Fair in our parish hall. Christmas shopping. I love wrapping Christmas presents up. Christmas decorations. Christmas cards. Christmas carols, Christmas films.

This year my friends and I are going to do our Christmas shopping together in the Square. We've bought most of our presents already, but I have to buy presents for my friends, and anyway, it'll be fun, all of us shopping together and then going into McDonald's or Burger King. Well, we think we will, anyway. Actually, more to the point, Grace has planned out every tiny detail and has for the last three months, and we just nod and smile because it's easier than saying, "Hey, why don't we forget about it?" Grace seems to spend most of her life planning out things.

Tara's slumber party is going to be deadly. We always do fun stuff. Most of the crowd from school are going – me, Grace, Liz, Naomi, Caitlin. Nicole is in Donegal for her cousin's wedding, and Jenny's grounded for sneaking out to the disco last week. She wouldn't have got caught except afterwards Naomi produced some bottles of cider and Jenny got totally drunk and came back to her house wrecked. All the adults say Naomi's a bad influence on us, and they're probably right, but she's mad fun.

The phone rings, and I grab it. It's Liz. "I got a chain letter," she tells me in a panicky voice. "I have to send ten copies of it to people or else everyone I know is going to die." Liz is very superstitious and believes in telekinesis, psychic powers, astrology, and all that sort of crap that none of our friends will tolerate. She's also vegetarian, and doesn't eat crisps or sweets, and is always on a diet. Still, she's all right.

"Calm down, Liz," I tell her. What would my friends do in this situation, I wonder. Naomi would probably agree wholeheartedly and get Liz all worried. Caitlin and Nicole would tell her it was just a load of junk and tell her to throw it in the bin. Jenny and Grace would tell her that it wasn't serious but that she should probably send the letters anyway, just to make sure.

"It's just something people send to scare you," I tell her. "You know that. But I think you should send the letters, just to be safe, you know."

"Thanks, Danielle, you're the best," she says. "See you at the slumber party, all right?"

"Yeah. See ya."

I hang up and check my watch. Not long to go until the greatest slumber party in the world.

2

Rachel

I sling my bag over my shoulder and walk out to the red car waiting outside my house, trying to look as if I go to slumber parties all the time. The truth is, I've only been to a few, and that was when I was really young and all we did was watch videos, try to stay up all night and then fail. Danielle is always raving about what fun Tara's parties are, so things must have changed since then.

Danielle's friend, Caitlin, smiles at me from the back seat and I slide in beside her. Liz and her mother are in the front. Danielle slips in beside me. She looks pretty, as always. She's always whining about how awful she looks, but I think she must know how pretty she is, deep down.

"Are you giving anyone else a lift?" I ask Liz.

"Nope. No one else needs one. Nicole and Jenny can't come, and Grace and Naomi live just down the road from Tara."

I hope I'll remember who is who among Danielle's

friends. I still can't figure out why I was invited. I hardly know most of the girls, except Caitlin, who lives two doors down from us. Plus most of them are two years older than me, and I don't go to the same school as them.

Danielle's the social queen in our family, definitely. She has loads of friends and she's always going off to discos and parties and everything. She's really popular at school and spends most of her time on the phone. I'm always upstairs studying because, basically, I have nothing better to do. I go to a private school miles away and all my friends live ages away from me. We hardly ever talk on the phone, either.

The car stops outside Tara's house and we all scramble out. We hurry up the driveway and ring the doorbell. Tara answers.

"Hi, everyone!" she squeals. "Grace is already here, planning out exactly what we're going to do all night."

"Sounds like Grace all right," Caitlin chuckles.

"Come on up!" Tara invites. We all thunder up the stairs and enter her room. It's huge. There's definitely enough room for us all to stay in here tonight. She has sleeping bags laid out already for us. I flop down on one at the edge, beside Caitlin. She stretches out luxuriously and then sits up. I smile at her.

"When did Naomi say she'd be here?" Danielle asks Tara.

"I told her 7:00, same as I told you," she replies. "But you know Naomi, she's never on time."

Naomi . . . which one is she, I wonder. Always late . . . oh, she's the one Mum says is a bad influence on Danielle. The small blonde-haired one.

I look around at the girls in the room. It's like being in *Sugar* or something. They're all so bubbly and confident and pretty. I feel completely left out. I busy myself organising the things in my bag beside my sleeping bag.

"I think we should watch *Titanic*," Grace says.

"Everyone's seen that millions of times," Tara protests. "And it's so long. How about *Scream 2*?"

They start arguing over which to watch. "What do you think, Rachel?" Caitlin asks me.

I don't have a clue. "Well, I've seen *Titanic* ten times and I don't really want to watch it again, and I haven't seen *Scream 2* at all."

"You haven't seen *Scream 2*?" Tara says incredulously.

"So what?" Caitlin sticks up for me, and I'm glad. She's really nice. "I haven't seen it either."

"I guess we'll be the only two actually enjoying it, then," I murmur to Caitlin.

She nods in agreement.

Tara turns on her CD player and a song begins to blare out of the speakers. It's killing my ears but I don't want to say so.

Through the loud noise I hear the doorbell. It must be Naomi. Sure enough, she comes into the room a few minutes later. She shows us a packet of cigarettes and a lighter she has hidden in her bag as well as several bottles of beer. I feel alarmed.

"Oh, God, Naomi, what'd you bring those for?" Tara sounds really annoyed. "I'm still in trouble with my parents over the disco last week. If they catch us drinking in here, I'm dead."

"They won't catch us," Naomi replies breezily.

"Forget it, Naomi. It's not worth it," Caitlin says.

I am quickly learning that there actually is a way to say "no" to alcohol and at the same time still be cool. Amazing.

"Just let me have one. Come on," begs Naomi. Without waiting for an answer, she lights a cigarette and expertly begins to smoke it. Caitlin coughs pointedly. Naomi ignores her.

Tara insists that Naomi puts the drinks away, which she reluctantly does, and Caitlin turns to me and rolls her eyes. "Every time," she smiles.

3

Danielle

We all crowd onto the couch in Tara's sitting-room, laughing. Caitlin is sitting on the armrest, and then Tara, Grace, Liz, Naomi and me are squeezed onto the couch. Rachel is sitting on the floor in front of Caitlin, who is playing with Rachel's hair.

The video begins to play. We start munching and drinking. We all have a can of Coke, a packet of crisps and some packets of sweets balanced on our knees.

We start to watch *Scream 2* in silence. Well, except for Naomi laughing occasionally. Every time she laughs, we all turn to her and tell her to shut up. Eventually we just give up and most of us start talking quietly.

We all scream in unison at a certain part and then we break into laughter. I'm having a great time. Rachel isn't showing off how brainy she is, and she isn't embarrassing me. She's getting along really well with Caitlin. I hope Caitlin is just being her usual friendly self and not actually becoming friends with Rachel.

The film is totally crap, and I've seen it loads of times before, but it doesn't really matter – only Caitlin and Rachel are paying attention.

"This is crap," Naomi whispers to me. "Have you ever seen a worse film?"

"Remember the time we saw *Mrs Brown*?" I ask her.

She screeches with laughter. "Oh, my God! That was horrible!"

"We were the only ones in the cinema under forty!" I add.

"Shut up!" Tara whispers to us.

When the film is over we all scramble upstairs. It's ten o'clock by then and Grace asks what are we going to do next.

"How about Truth or Dare?" suggests Naomi, grinning.

She *would* suggest it. She loves embarrassing us all.

"Great!" Grace says. "You can ask me first."

"I'll ask," Liz volunteers. "Truth or Dare?"

"Truth," Grace says.

"Okay . . . did you *really* meet Robbie at the disco?" Liz grins.

Grace looks very uncomfortable. So does Rachel, I notice. She's probably worried about being asked about meeting someone. I know for a fact she never has.

Grace sighs. "Yeah," she whispers. I don't see what the problem is here. Robbie's really nice. He's just not as cool as, say, maybe Mark or Adam or one of those guys, but he's sound.

Tara pretends to throw up. Liz pretends to gag. Naomi

makes a face. Grace starts to look really upset, but they don't notice and start slagging her off. Finally she bursts into tears and runs out.

"What'd you do that for?" Caitlin snaps at them. She's angry. She hardly ever is. I wonder if it's because she and Grace are really close or because she fancies Robbie.

"Why'd you have to be so bitchy?" I ask them.

Rachel looks distinctly uncomfortable and sits there quietly.

Caitlin leaves the room and I can hear her comforting Grace outside.

Liz, Tara and Naomi look as if they're feeling guilty. They should. Sometimes they just don't know when to stop, especially Naomi. Okay, so she's practically my best friend, but she can get so bitchy sometimes! Other times, though, she's the best friend you could ask for.

Grace marches back in, her eyes red. Well, not exactly red, but you can tell she's been crying. Still, she glares at the three wicked witches. "Truth or Dare?" she asks Naomi.

"Truth," Naomi replies. She looks surprised.

Grace smiles over at Caitlin, who has come back in. "Why," Grace begins, "did you tell us you'd met loads of boys when you haven't?"

For what is probably the first time in her life, Naomi is blushing furiously and I feel like cheering for Grace. I've a feeling Naomi is kicking herself for telling Grace about that. She's always going on about all the fellas she's met, but she makes most of it up.

Naomi starts to sulk and doesn't participate in the game.

We ignore her and continue playing. We're used to her being moody.

When it comes to Rachel's turn, she chooses a dare. I'm stunned.

"I dare you to phone my brother and get him to ask you out," says Liz. "Tell him you're in one of his classes. He doesn't have a clue who's in them. Go on."

She's not going to take it. It's impossible. She can't do it.

She walks over to the phone and asks Liz for her phone number. She dials and waits. "Hi, is Steve there?" she asks in a casual tone. She sounds much older than she is. I'm impressed.

"Hiya, Steve," she says. "I'm in your Irish class and I was out today . . . the teacher told me to get the homework off you, seeing as you're such a great student . . . oh, don't be modest, Steve, you know you are. Anyway, could I maybe get it off you during the weekend, maybe tomorrow . . ." She pauses. "Oh, Steve, you're the best. Really you are. So I'll see you in Burger King tomorrow, three-thirty, okay? Great. See you then." She hangs up. We're all staring at her in shock.

"How did you *do* that?" Liz asks in shock.

Rachel shrugs modestly, and as my friends begin gushing over her, I feel a familiar pang of jealousy.

***

It's nearly seven-thirty and we're still up. Caitlin is yawning and Liz is about to fall asleep. Naomi is in a better mood now and she is using her excellent make-up skills to make me, Rachel, Grace and Tara brilliant. Caitlin and Liz are on the other side of the room, doing each other's hair.

The room is littered with empty packets and cans, and I'm glad I'm not the one who'll be tidying it up. We've been having a great time all night. We made about a hundred prank phone calls, tried on all of Tara's clothes, played every CD she has, and generally just messed around.

Another five hours before we go home. Personally, I can't wait to get Rachel away from my friends.

4

Rachel

"So how was the party?" Siobhán asks on Monday morning when I arrive in school.

"It was okay," I reply. I have mixed feelings about it. Some of the stuff we did was really fun and great and I loved it, but other times I was so bored and thought the whole thing was just so ridiculous.

Siobhán and I walk into the classroom together. We sit alphabetically. As her last name is Cooper and mine is Connolly we sit together. She's really nice.

Julie joins us. The two of them are my best friends in school. There's another girl, Lauren, that we're really good friends with as well. Julie is tall and blonde and Siobhán is petite and dark-haired. Julie's hair is cropped short, like Danielle's, and Siobhán's is shoulder-length. They're always saying how lucky I am to have long hair, but sometimes it gets annoying.

"How was the slumber party?" asks Julie.

"We've been though this," Siobhán says. "She says it was okay."

"What did you do?" Julie asks.

I shrug. "We watched *Scream 2* and then we played Truth or Dare? and made joke phone calls, you know, the usual. To tell you the truth, half the time I didn't have a clue what they were talking about. They all go to the community school and were talking about all the boys they've met and everything."

Julie makes a sympathetic face. "And you felt totally out of place, right?" she says knowingly.

I nod. "Well, one of the girls, Caitlin, lives on our road, so I know her really well, and she's really nice. But the rest of them . . . well, I hardly knew any of them."

"Except Danielle," Siobhán reminds me.

"Like I said, I hardly knew any of them," I reply, and the three of us laugh.

"Is she really that bad?" Julie asks.

"It's not that she's bad. It's just that we have nothing in common," I explain. "Like, she doesn't care about school, and she's deadly at PE, and she's really popular and she's always out at discos and everything."

"And she's really pretty," adds Siobhán, who has been to my house and met Danielle.

"Thanks," I say sulkily. Even my friends think Danielle's the greatest. They don't have to shove it in my face.

"Come on, you know you're pretty as well," Julie reassures me.

"It's just that Danielle really cares about how she looks, and puts on make-up and stuff," Siobhán explains.

The warning bell rings. We hurry to get our books. First we have science. We're doing biology this term. I hate it when we have to dissect things. I like learning about organs and stuff, but in the book – not touching them and cutting them up! Julie is in a great mood. She loves science. She wants to be a nurse when she's older, so I guess she'll need it.

The door of the locker room swings open and I look over to see who it is. Lauren is trying to look as if she's not crying, but it's obvious she is. The wind has made her cheeks red and her strawberry-blonde hair is all over the place, making her look totally wrecked.

"My life is over," she declares dramatically as she joins us at our lockers. Lauren can be a bit over-dramatic at times.

"What happened, Laur?" Julie asks gently.

"I phoned him last night and he was out. His mum said he was out with his friends playing football, but I know he was with her, I just know it." She sobs even more loudly.

We've been filled in on the Lauren-Carl relationship. She loves him, he says he loves her, but Lauren is extremely paranoid and thinks he likes another girl, Kelly. Lauren has a tendency to exaggerate everything.

"Oh, Lauren, don't think that," Julie says soothingly, putting an arm around her while rolling her eyes at us as if to say *Not again!* Lauren has a crisis at least once a week and we're getting pretty sick of it by now.

Siobhán adds, "And if he *is* going with her, he's not worth it, then, is he?"

"No," Lauren sniffs, and then dries her eyes and almost instantly cheers up. "So, what do we have first class?"

She's very unpredictable. Julie looks at me and tries not to laugh while Lauren heads off to her locker.

***

"Did *anyone* get the answer right?" Ms Lynch asks in maths class. She looks very frustrated. We're doing a particularly hard section in maths and our class is taking ages to figure it out.

I raise my hand, expecting more to join me. Instead, everyone looks at me incredulously. "How did you *do* that, Rachel?" Julie asks me, twisting around in her seat to face me.

I shrug modestly. Secretly I'm pleased I've picked it up so fast.

"Well done, Rachel," Ms Lynch says. "As for the rest of you, I'll go over it once more. Rachel, you go ahead with the next question."

I begin working on the question while Ms Lynch keeps on talking. At the end of the class, she announces that there's going to be a test on this chapter on Friday.

"Bet you'll get a hundred per cent," Lauren says as she passes by me, and she says it with a bit of hostility rather than friendliness.

Being smart means school is easier for me, but I'd much prefer to feel more secure with my friends. Siobhán and Julie don't make a big deal out of me being smart, but Lauren can really get obnoxious about it sometimes. Why can't I be like Danielle, I wonder. She never has problems with her friends.

5

Danielle

Break finally arrives. Caitlin has been yawning ever since school started.

"I'm knackered," she groans, getting her books from her locker.

"Hi, Caitlin, hi, Danielle," says Robbie as he walks past her to his locker.

"Hi," she replies. Then she turns to me. "Did you think that he meant 'hi' as in, 'hi I love you', or 'hi' as in 'hi my good reliable friend'?"

"Caitlin, quit worrying about it," I tell her. "The Christmas disco is coming up soon, and we'll set you up with him."

Caitlin sighs. She's the quietest of our crowd and very friendly and kind, so I don't see why Robbie wouldn't like her.

Liz joins us. "My horoscope says this is my lucky love day," she reports.

I snort. "You don't really believe that crap, do you?"

"Why not?" she shrugs. Her locker is right beside mine, and she starts getting her books out.

I can think of about a million reasons why not, but decide it's not worth it. She won't listen, anyway.

Mark and Adam from our class stop beside us. "Hi," they say, and we respond.

There's a silence. "Guys," I say, "is there a reason we're all standing here doing nothing?"

"Robbie wants to know if you'll dance with him at the disco," Mark says.

I think that's a bit soon, seeing as the disco's on the Friday of next week, in twelve days' time, but I suppose he must be really eager. I turn to Caitlin to see what she's going to say. She glares at me and slams her locker shut. Gathering up her books, she storms off, looking close to tears.

"Well, will you?" Adam asks.

Oh my God, he's talking to me. To me.

I lean back against my locker. "Guys, I can't!" I exclaim. "Caitlin really likes him! I'm not going to do that to her!"

Adam looks as if he thinks that's the stupidest thing he's ever heard, but Mark looks as if he actually understands. Of course, he is the nicest guy in second year. "We'll tell him that," Mark says. "And I hope Caitlin isn't too pissed off with you."

"Thanks," I call after him. Then I turn to Liz. "I can't believe that just happened."

"I can," Liz replies. "It said in your horoscope something awful would happen to you today."

"Why didn't you tell me?" I want to know.

"You don't believe in horoscopes," she replies and then walks off. I'm left standing on my own, clutching my books to my chest, in the middle of a crowded hall.

I can hear two girls hollering my name. It must be Naomi and Nicole – they're the two loudest people I know. They push their way through the crowd and as soon as they reach me, I tell them what happened with Caitlin.

"Oh, God, what are you going to do?" Nicole asks.

"I don't know," I sigh, and I realise I have a big lump in my throat and tears are forming in my eyes.

"Oh, don't get upset about it," Naomi says. "Caitlin'll get over it."

I wish I could be that sure about it myself. Normally if I had a problem with a friend, I'd talk to Caitlin about it, but obviously that isn't an option. I suppose Grace is closest to her, apart from me, but I've a feeling Grace is going to be just as mad as Caitlin is about it. I run through my friends in my mind, wondering who could tactfully make Caitlin feel as if she should be annoyed with Robbie, and not me, but my friends are not exactly known for their tact. There's one person I can think of who could do it, if I asked her, but I'm reluctant to consider that option.

Nicole, Naomi and I walk down the corridor and Caitlin comes out of the girls' bathroom, her eyes red. Grace follows. Both of them glare at me and then walk off. We don't follow.

I decide I'll ask Rachel to talk to Caitlin and make her see sense.

***

We have double science last class. I hate it. "I really don't want to do this," moans Nicole. She, Naomi, Jenny and I are standing at our lockers chatting. Science has already started, but who cares if we're late?

"I hate biology," Jenny complains.

"Caitlin's my lab partner," I groan. "Oh, God, what'm I going to do?" It only takes me a few minutes to decide. "I'm not going," I announce. "Will one of you skip it with me or else I'll just go straight home."

"I will," offers Nicole.

"I'd better not," says Jenny. "Me and Naomi mitched two afternoons last week and I think they're getting suspicious."

"Only twice last week? Is that a record?" Nicole asks sarcastically. "Of *course* they're getting suspicious. You spend more time on the hop than you do in school."

It's true. Jenny and Naomi are always mitching. The rest of us don't. In fact this is the first time I'm ever going to skip a class. Well, this term, anyway.

"I'll say you're at the dentist," Naomi says to me, and to Nicole, "and I'll tell her you went home because you were sick. If she even notices you're gone."

"Thanks," we chorus. Jenny and Naomi hurry off to science. Nicole and I shove our books back into our lockers, get our coats and bags, and head out of the school. The principal's office faces the gate, so we slip out around the back way. It's private property and you're not supposed to go through there, but it's the only way to avoid getting caught.

"Do you want to go to my house?" Nicole offers. "It's closer, and my parents are at work."

"Okay," I agree, and we rush across the main road and hurry down the road to her house.

6

Rachel

Danielle arrives home late. She finishes at the same time as me, and it only takes her five minutes to get home, and it takes me longer as I have to wait for Mum and then wait in the traffic, but she must be hanging around with her friends all the time, because she usually gets home at the same time as me.

"I was at Nicole's," she tells me.

"Just for fifteen minutes?" I ask.

"*No*. We mitched double science."

"You skipped classes?"

"Well, *duh*."

"Sor-ry. I was only *asking*." I'm shocked. Mitching classes is a pretty stupid thing to do, and in our school you get immediate suspension for it. I'm guessing the punishment must be pretty similar at Danielle's school.

"Anyway, I need you to do me a favour," Danielle continues.

"Why should I?" I snap.

"Because you're my sister?" she tries. "Oh, come on, Rachel, do this for me, just one thing."

"Fine, what is it?" I relent.

"Go call for Caitlin," she says. "And talk some sense into her."

"What happened?"

She flops down on my bed and sighs. "Today at lunch, these guys come up to me and Caitlin and ask me will I dance with this guy, Robbie, at the Christmas disco. Caitlin fancies him, you see, and she got really pissed off that he likes me and not her, so now Caitlin hates me, and so does Grace, and I think Liz is on her side as well, and then Nicole, Naomi and Jenny are taking my side, so it's just one big mess and it's not even any of our faults. It's all because of Robbie." She pauses before continuing. "That's why I skipped science. Caitlin's my lab partner and now she hates me, so I didn't think I could cope with it. Nicole and I went to her house."

"What did you do there?" I ask curiously. I feel like a total moron, having to ask, but I really want to know what people *do* when they mitch.

"Just watched TV, talked about Robbie and stuff. You know, the usual," she says, looking surprised that I asked. "Anyway, I need you to talk to Caitlin and get her blaming Robbie instead of me."

"No way." I don't know Caitlin well to call for her, and I don't know how I'd get her feeling angry with Robbie, and I just don't want to get involved in this. And a part of me, a horrible part, actually likes seeing Danielle with a problem.

"Please . . ." she begs. "She'll listen to you, she likes you."

"No!"

"Come on . . . please . . ."

"Okay, okay, I'll go down, but if I don't manage to change her mind you can't get annoyed with me, all right?"

"Fine. Thanks. Great."

I change out of my school uniform. It's burgundy with a long pleated skirt, a horrible baggy jumper, and a disgusting tie. I wish I had Danielle's uniform. She's still sitting on my bed, running her hands through her hair as I get dressed. Her grey skirt is knee-length, and she rolls it up at the waist so it's a good bit further up her thigh. Her navy jumper actually fits well, and her sleeves are pushed up so even in her school uniform she manages to look casual and cool. I'm incredibly jealous.

I put on my jeans and a plain white T-shirt. "Do you want to wear my Adidas top?" offers Danielle.

I nod, surprised, and she runs to get it from her room. She must really want to keep on my good side. It makes a pleasant change. She returns carrying a black jacket with three white stripes down either side. I slip it on.

"Remember, don't make it seem like I sent you there," Danielle reminds me as I leave the house. I ignore her and jog down the road to Caitlin's house.

Caitlin answers the door. She looks upset and angry.

"Hi," I say tentatively, feeling awkward.

She smiles slightly. "Hi, Rachel. You want to come in?"

We sit down in the otherwise empty sitting-room. "So, what's up?" I ask her casually.

"I'm pretty sure Danielle's told you already," she scowls. "She's so pretty and popular, all the boys like her. It's not fair. She doesn't even care about Robbie, but I do, I really do."

"But it's not her fault," I say. "She can't help it."

"Yeah, right, she can't, going around like she owns the place, looking great all the time, herself and Nicole and Naomi. I hate all of them."

"Come on, Caitlin. You don't mean that. Are you going to let some boy get between you and your friends? Are you?" I'm not sure I'm saying the right things, but who cares, anyway. I know exactly what Caitlin's talking about, and it's hard not to completely agree with her, because I'm totally jealous of Danielle too, and I know that if I was in Caitlin's position I'd react exactly the same way. It's hard trying to change her mind because it means going against what I think.

"But God, Rachel, he's not just any boy. He's really nice and sensitive, and I really thought he liked me." She sniffs a bit. I feel awful. She's going to start crying any minute now.

"Maybe he just needs to get to know you," I suggest.

"He didn't need to get to know Danielle," she snaps. No, I'm wrong, she's not going to cry. She's angry, angry at everything and everyone, and I hope that doesn't include me.

"You know, Rachel, I'm really not good company right

now . . ." she begins. "Maybe you should just go home and I'll see you tomorrow or something, okay?" Well, at least she's being civil.

"Fine. See you." I try not to sound kind of insulted. I leave the house and hurry back home. I toss Danielle's top on her bed and storm into my room.

7

Danielle

"You left your second pair of earrings in," Nicole reminds me the next morning as we hurry into school the next morning. We both forgot we had assembly right before school and we're going to be late. I take off my silver hoops, leaving only my dolphin-shaped studs, and Nicole hides her purple-varnished nails behind her back as we enter the hall.

Mr Traynor, the vice-principal, is already there, talking to the other hundred or so second-year students, his back to us. We try to creep in, but he notices us.

"Ah, Miss Connolly, Miss Robinson," he says. "This is the second week in a row you've been late for assembly. Stay behind afterwards for late slips."

We look at each and groan silently as we sit down on a bench beside Naomi and Jenny. "We were late too," Naomi whispers across to us. "He's really pissed off with the four of us, I think."

"No wonder," I whisper back. "D'you think he knows about the mitching?"

"I hope not," Jenny says quietly. "If I get suspended, I'm dead."

She would be, too, if they ever find out about her and Naomi, since they mitch so often. Nicole and I might be let off with detentions, if we're lucky. I'm hoping it won't come to that. It'd just be my luck, wouldn't it, first time skipping a class this term and getting caught.

"You four, over there!" Mr Traynor barks. He means us. "If I catch you talking again, that's a black mark for each of you."

When he turns away, we all turn to each other and grin. We keep looking at each other as Mr Traynor drones on about school rules and exams, and eventually we burst into laughter – you know the way it's funny when you're all looking at each other but not talking.

"A black mark for each of you as well as a late slip!" Mr Traynor snaps. "I want to talk to you four after this."

Nicole starts playing with her long blonde hair. "I'm in such deep shit," she whispers to me. "I got a late slip yesterday as well, so with these ones that means I've got a detention, and I got one last week as well. If I get another detention I could get suspended!" She had three the term before as well. It takes six to get suspended. Since it takes only three black marks or late slips – they're the same thing, basically, except for what you get them for – to get a detention, it's pretty easy to end up there.

I make a sympathetic face. I'm in the same situation. I had a detention two weeks ago – plus three from before the mid-term break – and with a black mark from last week for

29

not doing my homework, I have another one. Just great. What will my parents say about *that*? They'll probably ask me why I can't be more like Rachel.

***

"Girls, this is not the first time you've created a distraction at assembly," begins Mr Traynor sternly.

Assembly is finished. My friends and I are standing beside the wall and he is pacing from Nicole, at one end of the line, to Naomi, at the other. We're all trying very hard not to laugh, because if we do, we're definitely dead. For most of us, this means trouble. Jenny only needs one more black mark for her sixth detention this term and therefore two-day suspension. Nicole and I need one more detention to get suspended, and naturally lucky Naomi is only on her second detention this term. She's so charming, she always manages to get out of getting into trouble, somehow.

The bell rings for the start of first class. Mr Traynor sighs. "I'll see you four in my office during break," he announces. "And you can tell your four cronies to come as well. I need to talk to them too."

We all know full well he means Tara, Grace, Liz and Caitlin, but still Naomi asks sweetly, "Who do you mean, Mr Traynor?"

"You know exactly who I am talking about," he says. "Tara Walsh, Grace Ryan, Liz McDonagh and Caitlin Young. I'll see you all in my office. Get to class now."

We all walk calmly out of the hall, but as soon as we're out of sight we start running. We're going to be late for class, and we don't even have our books out of our lockers. Life couldn't be better.

***

"Girls, you're late," we are gently reprimanded as we arrive in maths ten minutes late.

"Sorry, Ms Crowley," we chorus.

Naomi adds, "Mr Traynor wanted to talk to us after assembly and we didn't have time beforehand to get our books." She looks innocent and angelic. If only they knew!

"Well, seeing as that's the case, I'll let you off this time, but next time it's a late slip."

We exchange relieved glances as we slide into our seats at the back of the room. Tara is already in the seat beside mine. I tell her about going to the office at break.

"Shit," she mutters. "Why do *we* have to go up? I wasn't late. Not this time, anyway."

"He thinks we're all juvenile delinquents, apparently. He said some crap about disturbing classes and stuff like that."

"Why'd you skip science yesterday?" she whispers, suddenly remembering.

"Caitlin's my lab partner," I remind her. "Did you hear about what happened?"

"No, no one told me. You and Nicole weren't there, and everyone else was really huffy with the rest of us. What happened?"

I see that Ms Crowley has noticed us talking, so I scribble it down instead and pass it to Tara.

She writes back: *That's not fair, though. First of all it's not fair for either of you to drag the rest of us into it, and it's not fair for Caitlin to blame you for what Robbie thinks, but it's also not fair that Robbie likes you and barely notices Caitlin, is it? I'm not taking sides or anything. It's just I can see both points of view.*

I smile half-heartedly across at her and then fold the sheet of paper into quarters and tuck it into my pocket. Then I rest my chin on my hand and stare gloomily ahead.

***

Just before break, there's an announcement over the barely-working intercom system. "Could the following students come to Mr Traynor's office at break: Danielle Connolly, Nicole Robinson, Naomi Devlin, Jennifer Williamson, Tara Walsh, Grace Ryan, Elizabeth McDonagh and Caitlin Young."

We trudge up to the office at break. I'm starving. I was in such a rush I had no breakfast, and I feel really weird – sort of weak. God, I hope I don't faint or anything.

"Are you okay?" Tara asks me on our way down the corridor. "You look really pale."

"Yeah, you do," agrees Nicole. "Do you feel sick or anything?"

I shake my head. It instantly gives me a headache. "I just need to eat, that's all. I'm starving."

We troop into Mr Traynor's office. Nicole, Naomi, Jenny and I are on one side, and Caitlin, Liz, and Grace are on the other. Tara is kind of hanging in between. If I wasn't so depressed about us all fighting, I'd find it funny.

"Now, girls, I'm sure you all know why you're here," he begins.

We all nod meekly.

"Girls, I have been getting bad reports of you ever since the start of the year from all the teachers, and last year you were getting into trouble as well. This has to stop. You're constantly late for class, and I've heard that several of you appear to be absent without a reason from afternoon classes frequently." He pauses and looks around at all of us. I glance around. Grace looks like she's about to cry. Jenny is trying not to laugh. Tara is biting her nails. Naomi is gazing innocently at him.

"You can wipe that angelic look off your face, Miss Devlin," he snaps. Naomi tries to look hurt and upset.

"Anyway," Mr Traynor says, "I am, frankly, fed up with hearing about the eight of you."

"That's not fair," Nicole exclaims.

Mr Traynor frowns. "What isn't fair, Miss Robinson?" he asks, looking disapproving.

"You're blaming all of us just because we're all friends, but Caitlin and Grace and Liz and Tara don't do anything. They're always on time and always have their homework done and everything. It's not fair to be giving out to them because they haven't done anything." She stares defiantly at him. I exchange worried looks with Naomi. Not the way to talk to the vice-principal, I think. Nicole is going to be in so much trouble. I fully approve of assertiveness and saying what you think – in theory, anyway. Not when you're practically screaming it at your vice-principal.

"That's a detention for you," he snaps. "You don't give cheek to your teachers. Now, if I'm right, that will have to be after the detention you got this morning, and won't this be your sixth detention this term?"

Nicole nods.

"That's a two-day suspension," he reminds her.

"Yes, Mr Traynor," she says. As he turns around, she makes a face at his back.

I surreptitiously check my watch. Break time's nearly over.

Mr Traynor gives Nicole a letter for her parents and then returns to talking to all of us. "If I hear one more report of bad behaviour from any of you, you're *all* going to be suspended."

This is so unfair, I think, but I know not to speak up. I'll just get into more trouble.

"You can go now," he says, leaving us about two minutes to have some lunch and get our books.

We all walk out of the office. Grace, Liz, Tara, and Caitlin hurry off down to the lockers first, and the rest of us go down to the classroom to have our lunch.

"I hate him," snaps Nicole as we enter the classroom. "I was just telling the truth! He's blaming all of us instead of just us four. I just told him that, and he gives me a detention. What a bastard! My mum's going to kill me."

"I can't believe that only one of us has to do something wrong for all of us to get suspended," moans Jenny. "That's such shit."

"I think I'd prefer just to get suspended and have it over with," I volunteer. "I mean, we're going to be creeping around here, rushing everywhere, trying not to get into trouble, but if all it takes is one thing, we're going to get suspended anyway. We might as well just get it over with and then it'll take another eighteen black marks to get another suspension."

"You're probably right," Naomi says, "but I'd prefer to try to avoid it altogether."

"Hey," Mark greets us as he sits down beside us. "You get into trouble?"

"I'm fucking suspended," Nicole informs him, waving the letter in the air.

"Not only that," Naomi continues, "but if any of us does one thing wrong, we're all going to get suspended."

"Well, if you are, you can always come to me . . ." he offers. Jenny hits him on the shoulder and makes a face at him.

I grab my lunch and start eating hungrily.

"Yeah, that's right. Stuff your face, Danielle," Mark says.

"Shut up, I didn't have any breakfast," I retort. I feel dizzy for a second and have to put my head down.

"Are you all right?" asks Mark, putting his arm around me. I shrug it off automatically even though it feels sort of nice, comforting.

"Leave it, you pervert," snaps Naomi.

I raise my head. "I'm fine, seriously," I reassure them.

"Are you sure?" Nicole asks.

I begin munching my lunch again. The bell sounds for the start of class. "Oh, shit," I mutter. "I haven't even gotten my books out yet." I gaze adoringly at Mark. "Would you . . ."

"Sure," he says good-naturedly.

I toss him my keys. "I need my home ec book and my two home ec copies, okay? It's number two fifty-eight."

He goes out of the room.

"You know he's mad about you," Nicole says.

I shrug. "He's not. We're just friends, you know that."

"Yeah, sure," Naomi snorts. "Whatever you say . . ."

8

Rachel

"Get the ball, Rachel!" screams Julie during hockey practice at lunch.

I sprint over to where the ball is headed, outrunning the girl in the other team, and with my hockey stick hit the white ball over to Julie, who whacks it into the goal. Our team cheers.

Sports aren't really my thing, but since we have to play one, I picked hockey. Right now I'm playing midfield.

My watch says it's half-one. Only another five minutes of practice. Lauren is playing as well, but she spends most of her time playing with her hair.

Ms Hogan, one of the hockey coaches, lets us go early, and Julie, Lauren and I sprint back to the classroom. Siobhán, who couldn't go to hockey because she forgot her tracksuit, is sitting at her desk doing her homework.

"Hiya," she greets us when we come in.

I quickly pull off my burgundy and white school tracksuit

top and, leaving my white T-shirt on underneath, slip my cream blouse on and start buttoning it up. It's absolutely freezing these days and we all wear something underneath our blouses now.

All of us who have returned from hockey start getting changed into our uniforms. I'm glad my desk is beside the radiator, otherwise I'd be freezing. I left my uniform on it all through practice, so now it's lovely and warm.

When I'm dressed, I go to my locker and, leaving my tracksuit neatly folded up on the bottom of it, fetch my books for the rest of the day. The bell goes for the end of lunch, and we all moan.

We have CSPE next. First the roll is called. "Lauren Andrews?" Miss Killeen says.

Lauren hurries into the classroom, her books in her arms. "Sorry," she gasps, and slides into her place. She turns around to us and smiles.

"Julie Bennett?" Miss Killeen continues. Julie raises her hand.

I turn to Siobhán. "Did you remember to bring in your Amnesty International information?"

She nods.

"No talking, girls," Miss Killeen says automatically, and Siobhán and I turn to each other and smile.

***

After CSPE there's English. Miss Morgan has us for that. She gives us back the essays we had to write about "Winter". Right now she's talking about the ones she thinks were the best. Heather Connell's one is chosen, and so is mine. I'm asked to read mine aloud.

"When the brightly coloured autumn leaves begin to disappear from our paths and streets, and our mild weather grows colder, and the night seems to envelop most of the day, we know winter has arrived," I begin. "Cruel and merciless, it begins its three-month onslaught with sharp, cold winds and heavy showers of rain."

My face is hot and red. I hate reading my essays aloud.

Everyone claps when I'm finished. I blush even more.

"Great essay, Rachel," Lauren calls, but again I feel like she's angry with me.

PE is our last class. I change into my tracksuit for the second time today and so does the rest of the class. We hurry down to the PE hall. We're on the ropes again. They're really hard to get across. Climb up the frame, pull yourself over to the next frame using three ropes, then there's another three ropes to go across and then another frame, then you can get down.

Siobhán moves swiftly across, like a monkey. She's amazingly athletic. I follow her, moving slowly and cautiously. I manage to complete it, at least, and go to the back of the line waiting for my next turn.

I watch Lauren try to get across the second set of ropes. She slips off and hurries to the end of the line. "I'm so crap at this," she whines.

"No, you're not," Siobhán says. "You just need to keep on trying."

Easy for her to say, I think. I'd love to be as fit as she is.

When the class is over, most people have got across four times. Siobhán and I have both got across five times. Lauren has got across twice and seems to be really annoyed with me and Siobhán. I try to ignore her. Even though she's one of my friends, lately she hasn't exactly been friendly to me.

***

My mum is waiting for me in her car outside the school. I call bye to my friends and hop into the car. They stroll off down the road in a group, talking and laughing. I wish I was with them.

"We got our French tests back today," I say conversationally. "I got 90%."

"90%? Rachel, you know you can do better than that. What about all those after-school French classes you took in primary school? You should be getting 100%!"

"What?" I say in astonishment. "Are you telling me that although I got an A for my French test, and one of the best scores in the class, you're not satisfied? Is that what you're saying?"

"Rachel . . . you can do better than 90%. You know that."

I turn away and sulkily stare ahead. There's a big lump in my throat. She's being so unfair and unreasonable. I hate her, I think. I really and truly hate her.

9

Danielle

"Managed not to get into trouble all day," says Naomi, pleased with herself, on the way home.

"Nice for you," Nicole says, "but I'm suspended until Friday. I'm dead." She reaches her house and we stop. "If you never see me again, please tell Dónal Whelan I love him," she adds dramatically, referring to the boy in our class that she fancies.

"If you don't get grounded, we'll see you tomorrow," Naomi calls cheerfully as she and I head down the road.

"We just have to make it until Christmas," Naomi says, "without doing anything wrong. Then we can start over again." You have to get eighteen black marks in the same term. Once a new term starts the others are automatically cancelled.

"We have one more week until the start of the Christmas exams, exactly," I say, "and two weeks until we get our holidays. Can we manage that?"

"Probably not," she shrugs.

We're at my house now, and I call bye to her as she continues down the road.

Mum's car has just pulled into the driveway. Rachel gets out, looking sullen and upset and angry. Then Mum gets out, her expression neutral. I tell her I have detention on Friday along with Nicole, Jenny and Naomi.

Mum gets really annoyed. "Danielle, this is your second detention this term! Why can't you be more like your friend Caitlin? I've been talking to her mother, and Caitlin never gets into trouble, so why do you have to? I knew you shouldn't be hanging around those other girls. They're a bad influence on you. Naomi and what's-her-name . . ."

"Nicole," I mutter.

"Right, whatever." We all go into the house, Rachel stomping up to her room. "They're obviously the cause of this. I don't want you seeing any more of them."

"That isn't fair, Mum," I protest. "Naomi and Nicole are my friends and right now they're being better friends than Caitlin is. I'm not going to stop being friends with them just because you say so. You barely even know them!"

I'm angry. She doesn't know a thing about my friends, any of them. She doesn't know that Nicole gets really upset when she sees anyone smoking. She doesn't know that Naomi was so nice to me when my old boyfriend dumped me. She doesn't have a clue about any of my friends.

I storm up to my room. After a few moments I go into Rachel's room. She is on her bed, reading, but the force with which she is turning the pages, almost ripping them, suggests she is angry.

"Are you okay?" I ask.

"Oh, fine, just fine," she growls.

"Hey, you're not the only one," I snap. "I'm on the verge of getting suspended."

"Ask me if I care," she says.

"Bitch. I just wanted to talk."

"Ooh, great, let's *talk*, let's *bond*," she practically spits out.

"And I thought Caitlin was being a cow," I mutter.

"She is. Practically bit my head off yesterday. Add that to the fact that one of my best friends hates me, that I'm totally unathletic, and that my mum is annoyed because I did really well on my French test . . . oh, my life is just great."

"Hey, if any of my friends do one thing out of line we're all going to be suspended. Nicole already is, and add that to the fact that all of us are fighting and I feel like it's my fault . . ."

"Plus our mum's a bitch," adds Rachel.

I stare at her in shock. "*What* did you say?"

She looks back at me defiantly. "I *said* that our mum's a bitch."

I didn't even think Rachel *knew* how to say something like that. "Is that you, Rache? Where's Miss Sweet and Innocent, teacher's pet, Mummy's girl, Daddy's angel, huh?"

"I am so sick of having to be like that!" she exclaims. "I told Mum I got 90% in my French test, right? It was this really hard one that I spent ages studying for, and you know what she said? *You can do better.* God, if any one of my friends went home with a score like that they'd be praised for ages. But not me, I just get the *You can do better* speech."

43

"I hate Mum," I say. "Did you hear what she said about my friends? She thinks Nicole and Naomi are a bad influence on me."

"Nicole? Is she the one who's real paranoid about smoking? Caitlin said she was really nice. She sounds like it, too."

At that moment I absolutely love my sister for saying that.

"And Naomi!" Rachel continues. "Well, I can understand why Mum thinks what she does, but she seems okay."

"See! You barely know them either, but at least you're not accusing them of turning me into a juvenile delinquent or something."

"Danielle," she states flatly, "no one *needs* to turn you into one. You already *are* one."

I know she's kidding. At least I hope she is. She'd better be.

"So, when is your school's Christmas disco?" I ask her, changing the subject.

"Friday week, same as yours, but Mum and Dad have that dinner party to go to and I can't get a lift off anyone, so I'm not going."

"So come to our one," I suggest, hoping I won't regret this later. Right now I feel full of sisterly love. "You already know lots of my friends, and I'll introduce you to some of the boys and stuff. And I'll help you find an outfit! Come on, it'll be great!" Well, as close to great as you can get in our area. The discos themselves are crap, I'd prefer to go to Freedom or Taney or Wesley, but with all your friends there, it can get really fun.

"All right!" she agrees, grinning, and for the first time in ages we're getting along really well. I just hope it lasts.

10

Rachel

Wednesday morning, I wake up after dreaming about the disco. I can't wait to go to Danielle's one. It'll be my second disco, only. My first was our end-of-year disco at the end of sixth class, and that was ages ago. Danielle has agreed to let me borrow anything in her wardrobe except her own outfit. I've seen it, and there is no danger of me wanting to wear it. It's absolutely gorgeous, but it's just not me. She'll look great in it though.

"Hiya!" Danielle bounces in.

It's December, it's cold, it's an hour before Danielle even needs to get up to be at school on time. And yet she is bright and cheerful at 7:00 in the morning, and I am still hiding underneath the covers.

"It's not Christmas morning yet," I remind her sleepily as I pull myself out of bed.

"Only another eighteen days to go!" she replies cheerfully. She's counting the days and has been since the start of the school year.

She tosses my dressinggown over to me. I wrap it around me.

"It's too cold to be cheerful," I mutter, putting on my furry kitten-shaped slippers and trudging downstairs.

"Smile, Rache!" she says sweetly. "You look gorgeous when you smile. But I guess we have the same genes, huh?"

"Why are you so happy?" I ask. "I mean, you're probably going to get suspended soon and if that happens Mum and Dad will kill you, and ground you, so then you'll miss the Christmas disco and I won't have the guts to go without you, so we will both be miserable and then I will be really mad at you and probably end up throwing you out of the window in a homicidal rage."

"Yeah, but still . . ." She's still smiling. I don't understand it. My notoriously morning-grouch of an older sister who can't stand the cold and is usually very moody has got up an hour early on a freezing cold winter's day and is bubbly and bright. The world has indeed gone mad.

***

"I got my outfit for the Christmas disco yesterday," announces Lauren when I get into school. It seems like everyone's talking about the Christmas disco these days.

"I already have mine," Julie says. "Hey, Rachel, are you sure you can't go?"

"I'm sure," I reply. "I'm going to our local one instead with Danielle and her friends."

"So how is your sister, anyway?" Siohbán asks. She really likes Danielle.

"Her and all her friends are one black mark away from getting suspended," I offer. "Mum's really annoyed with her."

"I bet," Julie says. "My mum was really annoyed when I got *one* late slip."

"Oh, Rachel," Siobhán says, "I have those photos from when I was at your house at Halloween – remember when I slept over? They're in my locker."

"Great!" I say enthusiastically. "Will you get them?"

The four of us go into the locker room and she opens her locker and pulls out a pile of photos. We return to the classroom, and perched on various desks and chairs look through them. The first ones are of me and Siobhán together. She dressed up as a vampire and I was Morticia Adams – I put temporary colour in my hair to make it black.

Then there are some of the two of us with Danielle and Caitlin, who slept over as well. Danielle was a dancer, dressed in this exotic sort of light flimsy costume, and Caitlin was a witch. The four of us went out together, trick-or-treating, for the fun of it. It was particularly wet and cold that night, I remember, so there were very few people out. There were little groups of small kids running around, excited, and then there was us. It was terrific. Danielle was complaining of being freezing the whole time. Afterwards we went to the bonfire down the road and then we came back to watch *Scream*.

We had such a great time that night, I'm remembering it all now. There's a big smile on my face.

"Danielle is so pretty!" exclaims Lauren. "She's gorgeous."

For once I'm not annoyed. I find a photo of me and Danielle together, smiling and really happy.

"She looks so like you!" Julie exclaims. "I mean, her hair's the same colour and she has kind of the same face as you."

"Except that Danielle's really pretty," I say sweetly.

Siobhán looks at me like she's saying *Come ON . . .*

"So, what do we have first class?" Julie asks.

"Irish," I say.

I go my locker and get out my books. Lauren follows me. "I got Carl a ticket to the disco," she says, "but he might not be able to come. What'm I going to do then, Rachel?"

"I don't know," I say wearily. At this moment, my mind is not on my school's Christmas disco which all my friends will be at. It's on the community school's disco which I'll be going to and I'm thinking about all the fun I'm going to have with Danielle and her friends.

11

Danielle

I can't wait for lunch to be here. It's hard actually paying attention the whole time without messing or dossing. It's a new experience. Naomi came close to getting a black mark this morning but she managed to charm her way out of it. Thank God.

The bell finally rings for lunch. My friends and I all have lunch passes, which means we can leave the school to go home for lunch. Naomi, Jenny and I leave the school, showing our laminated passes to the sixth years who are manning the gates. Tara is playing basketball, and somehow I don't think the others will be spending lunchtime with us.

"Let's call for Nicole," I suggest. None of our parents will be at home, so there's no one worrying about us.

"Great idea," Jenny says. "She's probably grounded, so we'll only be able to see her at lunch when her parents aren't home."

We cross the road and ring Nicole's doorbell. She opens it, dressed in an Adidas tracksuit.

"Hiya!" we scream at her.

"Oh, hi!" she says. She sounds quieter than usual. That means not screaming out every single word. But she doesn't look as cheerful and energetic as she usually does, either.

"Are you all right?" I ask her.

"I'm grounded for a week," she says. "It could be worse, I suppose, and I'm still able to go to the disco. But listen to this – no phone for a week, either, or TV, or computer. Isn't that so unfair? I mean, I'm already suspended. My mum doesn't have to make me more miserable." She looks as if she's about to cry for a moment, but then she regains her composure and I think I must have imagined it. Come on, this is Nicole we're talking about. I don't think I've ever seen her upset since I've become friends with her, and that's a long time.

"So, you want something to eat?" she offers.

"Sure," Jenny says.

"Crackers and cheese okay?" she says as we follow her into the kitchen.

"Sure," Naomi says. "Hey, Nicole, you want us to stay all lunch?"

"I don't mind," she shrugs. I get that feeling again that she's upset.

"So, what've you been doing?" Nicole asks brightly. Now she's all bouncy again.

"Well, my sister is coming to our disco," I say.

"Really? Rachel? What's she like?" Nicole says.

"She's really nice," Naomi offers. "A bit quiet, though."

To Naomi, *everyone* is a bit quiet. Yelling is normal for her.

"She's thirteen, right?" Nicole says.

"Twelve," I correct.

"And she's in second year?"

"Mm-hmm. I told you, she started early and then got moved ahead."

"But still . . . when's her birthday?"

"September."

"Wow. That's young."

"*And* she's the best in her class," I say. For once, I'm proud of Rachel.

"Bet she spends all her time studying and never has any fun," says Nicole.

"Just like you," teases Naomi. We all know that to Nicole studying is an alien concept. Then Naomi continues, "But Rachel's not like that, though, is she? I mean, we had a deadly time with her at the slumber party."

"You spent half the slumber party sulking, Naomi," I remind her sweetly.

"Oh, shut up," Naomi says, shoving me. I push her back.

Nicole gets us all our crackers and cheese, and pours us all some Coke and tosses us some packs of crisps and mini Mars bars.

"If Liz was here she wouldn't eat a thing. She's on another diet," Jenny blurts out.

I really wish we weren't fighting with them.

"You're still fighting, huh?" Nicole says.

"Yeah," we chorus glumly.

Jenny adds, "Caitlin and Grace and Liz won't even talk to us, and Tara is starting to take their side too. I hate this. It's all Robbie's fault."

That may be true, but it feels like it's my fault. I know deep down it really isn't, but it's hard not to feel responsible for this big fight. I hate fighting with my friends. I hate it even more this time as Caitlin is always so nice.

There's a long silence for a while where we're just all looking at each other. Jenny is fiddling with her dark blonde hair. Then we all burst into laughter.

"Did you get the results of our Irish test back?" Nicole asks when we're finished laughing.

"No," replies Jenny. "We didn't get our science tests back either."

"Oh, remember what you said in science this morning?" Naomi says to Jenny. Naomi, Jenny and I all start laughing. I look over at Nicole. She's biting her nails.

"Jenny was asked to read in science today," I explain to Nicole. "We're doing biology now, as you know, and she read out 'organism' as 'orgasm'."

Nicole laughs.

"You should've heard her!" Naomi continues. She mimics Jenny, starting by pushing her hair behind her ears repeatedly just like Jenny does when she's asked to read. "And that is how the orgasm . . . uh, orgasmic . . . *organism* . . . produces energy . . ."

"Shut up, Naomi," Jenny is blushing. Naomi's always slagging her off. She's kidding most of the time but Naomi can be really mean sometimes, without realising it.

52

"Naomi, give her a break," Nicole says.

"Sure, Ms Rebel," Naomi says sweetly. "How's the life of a juvenile delinquent?"

"Fine," Nicole replies, suddenly gloomy.

"Are you sure you're all right?" Jenny asks with a concerned expression on her face.

"Just leave me alone, okay?" Nicole says quietly.

Naomi, Jenny and I exchange worried looks but don't speak, and start nibbling at our crisps to have something to do.

12

Rachel

"Why can't it be Christmas?" whines Lauren. Like Danielle, she's been wishing it was Christmas for the last three months.

"Because it's only the seventh of December?" suggests Julie sweetly. We're all getting a bit fed up with Lauren, I must say.

"At least we have tomorrow off!" says Siobhán happily. "I'll cycle down to see you, okay? And Danielle."

"Danielle's school isn't off tomorrow," I say. "Hey, why don't I cycle up here instead and we can call for Julie and Lauren?" I don't intend on calling for Lauren at all, but I can't exactly say that while she's around.

"Okay," she agrees.

Lunchtime has just finished. We've just come from studying at the library, and now we're back at the classroom. Some of the girls are rushing around finishing their lunch, getting books and finishing homework, others are sitting calmly in their places or chatting to their friends.

Rachel

I did all my homework in the library, so I leave my books back in my locker and get the ones I'll need for our last three classes. We have history, English and computers, three of my favourite subjects.

Lauren comes over to me. "What're you doing?" she says.

"Getting my books," I reply. She really annoys me sometimes but I don't know how to tell her to get lost. Danielle would, I think jealously. I'm not confident enough. She is. Stop thinking like that, I tell myself. Danielle's being really nice to me at the moment and for the first time in ages we're actually friends. And I love it when we are, and I'm going to do everything I can to make sure things stay this way.

***

Siobhán and Julie are on either side of me for computers. We're doing word processing – again. We spent lots of time on it last year and we're back on it again this year. Julie is brilliant at typing; her fingers are flying over the keypad. Siobhán and I are surreptitiously glancing down at the keys as we type slowly and carefully. We're on Mavis Beacon at the moment, and our scores come up when we're finished. Julie has 100% accuracy and 37 words per minute. Siobhán and I have almost identical results, with 90% accuracy and 15 and 18 words per minute respectively.

After computers I have a headache, as usual. The computer room is very stuffy and with nearly thirty computers around you, it's hard not to be affected. I'm also exhausted. It's been a long day. I yawn as my friends and I go down a flight of stairs to the ground floor of the school where all the second- and third-year classrooms are. The fifth- and sixth-year classrooms are on the top floor, and in between are the science labs, home ec rooms, the religion room, the language rooms, the supervision rooms and the library. The transition years are in a separate building that also has the PE and assembly hall in it, and the first-years are in a separate building. Lucky them.

We go down the corridor and into our classroom, and my gabardine and zipped-up schoolbag are waiting for me in my place. I put them on and, calling goodbye to my friends, head out of the school. My mum is listening to the car radio when I hop into the car. We drive off.

"I hope that sister of yours managed to stay out of trouble today," she mutters as we wait at the traffic lights.

So do I. It must be hard, though. I think of Naomi and the cigarettes at the slumber party. If she gets caught smoking or anything, the whole lot of them will get suspended. I think that's really unfair. Okay, so I don't really know that much about the situation, but I know it's not fair to blame eight girls for what one of them does. And I just can't imagine Grace and Caitlin and Liz as the type to always be getting into trouble.

"It's those girls she's friends with, I know it is," Mum continues. "Naomi and Nicole and Jennifer. If she just kept to Caitlin and Elizabeth she'd be fine."

Mum is so prejudiced. Why have I never noticed this before? She's blaming all Danielle's friends for Danielle getting into trouble. And that's not fair.

"Naomi's really nice," I speak up. "And Danielle says she's really smart." That's true. Danielle *did* say that. She also said that it was a pity Naomi spent more time mitching than she did in school, but I get the feeling it wouldn't be a good idea to mention that to Mum.

"That may be so, but I've also heard very distressing rumours about her," Mum says, barely taking in what I said.

"And Caitlin isn't as nice as you think she is," I continue hotly. "She was a real bitch to me yesterday."

"Rachel! Did you just say what I think you said?" Mum sounds shocked.

I decide to do what Danielle would do. "I said Caitlin was a real bitch to me yesterday," I say, trying to look defiant and rebellious. "And it's true."

"I don't want to hear that sort of language from you, young lady," Mum snaps.

"Okay, so it's all right for Danielle to say things like that but not me. Is that what you're saying?" I say huffily.

Mum starts talking about 'different expectations for both of you' and 'with your intelligence you don't need to use that sort of language' and that sort of stuff. I ignore her, and stare out the window. We're almost home. Once we are, I hurry up to my room. I'm fed up with my mother and her stupid ideas. I'm fed up with everything at the moment, but then Danielle arrives home, and I can hear her snapping at Mum when she enquires, "Did you manage to keep out of trouble today?" Then I hear Danielle's footsteps up the stairs and I feel better knowing that my sister is as sick of my mother as I am.

***

The phone rings. I get it. It's probably for Danielle, but she's in the shower.

"Hello?" I say.

"Hi, is Rachel there?" It's Siobhán.

"This *is* Rachel," I laugh.

"Oh, sorry!" she laughs. "It's just that you sounded really like Danielle." I'm not sure whether I'm pleased or annoyed.

"Anyway," she continues, "I called to tell you I have to go down to Wexford to see my relatives tomorrow, so I won't be able to call for you."

I'm disappointed, but try not to sound it. "Oh, well. I'll call for Julie, anyway."

"She's going shopping with her cousin all day – she told me on the way home from school. Sorry . . ."

"No, it's fine," I say. "Really."

"Okay, well, I'll see you on Friday."

"See you," I say, and then I slam down the phone angrily and try not to let the tears forming in my eyes trickle down my cheeks.

***

I'm cheered up when Michelle Norton calls around for me after school. Michelle and I were best friends in primary school, but now she's in a Gaelscoil three miles away. We try to see each other as much as possible, but it's hard, because she has so much stuff going on after school – speech and drama, piano lessons, recorder classes, flute practice, hockey, basketball and camogie training.

"How's life going?" she asks me brightly.

"Fine," I reply, "except for this stupid fight with Caitlin."

"Yeah, Eric said that Caitlin was being really moody today."

Eric's her brother, eleven months older than she is, who's in Danielle's class. He begged to go to their school, but Michelle adores Irish so she went to a different school. I used to fancy Eric a lot.

Michelle grins. "Oh, speaking of my brother who you fancy like mad . . ."

"I do not! That was ages ago!"

"Yeah, right. You know, he fancied you too. And . . . I think he still does."

"Whatever," I reply. "I really don't care."

13

Danielle

At dinner, things are very awkward. Rachel is quiet, I'm quiet, Mum is angry and quiet, and Dad is trying to start up a conversation. "How's school?" he asks me.

"Okay," I say neutrally.

He turns to Rachel. "Have a good day?"

"It was all right," she replies quietly.

Finally he gives up and we munch in silence. Rachel leaves first, I follow. We go into the sitting room and switch on the TV.

***

The next morning, Rachel is still sleeping by the time I drag myself out of bed. I wish *I* had the day off. I drink a cup of tea and then hurry out the door. School starts in five minutes. I run all the way and arrive just as the bell goes. Naomi has my spare locker key, she's already got my books out for me and is waiting with them outside the classroom.

She hands them to me and we hurry inside and sit down at the back of the classroom. Ms Desmond, our CSPE teacher, strides in a few seconds later, and her eyes sweep the room for any latecomers.

"I see Nicole is out," she says.

"She's suspended for two days," Naomi speaks up.

"I see." She marks this in her notebook.

Mark enters the classroom. "Sorry," he says, and sits down in front of me. He turns around at me and grins. I smile back.

"Mark, turn around," Ms Desmond says. He does so. She starts talking. A few minutes later he turns around to me again and starts talking.

"Mark and Danielle!" Ms Desmond is practically shrieking. "A black mark for both of you!"

I'm horrified. I can't get a black mark now. I'll get all my friends into trouble as well.

"Danielle wasn't talking," Mark speaks up. "I was. She wasn't doing anything."

"Then *you* can have *two* black marks," she says sweetly. He nods.

After class, I approach him. "Thank you *so* much," I say, hugging him. "You're the best."

"Want to get closer than that?" he asks mischievously.

I hit him on the shoulder. "Get lost," I laugh.

"She really wants me. She's just trying to hide it," he stage-whispers to Naomi. She snorts.

"You'd love my sister Rachel," I tell him. We begin to walk down to the lockers.

"Why? Does she look like you?" he asks.

"Rachel's *gorgeous*," Eric volunteers. His sister used to be Rachel's best friend until they went into different secondary schools.

"And she's really smart," I add.

"And really nice," puts in Naomi.

"And she's coming to our Christmas disco," I finish. "Will you dance with her?"

He shrugs. "Sure."

I smile at him. "Great." And it is, too. Rachel and Mark would be perfect together, I just know it.

***

Naomi, Jenny and I leave the school at lunchtime. I sprint home to get my geography copy with my homework in it. Rachel is sitting gloomily on the couch, watching TV.

"What're you doing home?" she asks. "They didn't throw you out, did they?"

"I'm just getting my geography homework." I retrieve the copy from the desk in the corner of the sitting room. "So, what're you doing?"

"Watching TV. I'm so bored. What're you going to do now?" She looks miserable. I feel sorry for her.

"Naomi and Jenny are waiting for me down the road. We're going to call for Nicole. She's grounded so we can only see her at lunch. Want to come with us?"

"But what about your friends?" She has a hopeful look on her face.

"They won't mind," I reassure her.

"Okay, well, if you're sure . . ."

"Oh, just come *on*, Rachel!"

She grins and jumps up. She slips her keys into her jeans pocket and we leave.

Naomi and Jenny are waiting at the corner. I roll up the copy into a cylinder shape and slip it into my jacket pocket.

"Hi," I greet them.

"Hi, Rachel," Naomi says.

"Hi," she replies.

"This is Rachel, this is Jenny," I introduce them with a wave of my hand.

"Hi," they both chorus.

"Are you coming with us to Nicole's?" Naomi asks.

Rachel nods.

We start to walk down the road. Naomi lights a cigarette and starts smoking it. We reach Nicole's house. "Don't ring the doorbell yet –" Naomi says, but it's too late. Jenny already has. Naomi inhales the smoke.

Nicole answers the door. Her eyes immediately focus on the wisp of smoke floating upwards from Naomi's cigarette. Nicole hates smoking with a passion.

"Put it out, Naomi," she says quietly.

"In a minute," Naomi says carelessly

"Now." Her voice is tense and strained.

"In a second!"

Nicole reaches over and grabs it out of Naomi's hand. She drops it on the ground and extinguishes it with a stamp of her foot. "Come on in," she says calmly.

We all file in. "Are you all right?" I whisper.

She nods and turns to Rachel. "So, you're Rachel?"

"Yeah," Rachel replies. "Last time I checked, anyway."

Nicole laughs. "So, you want to go up to my room?" she suggests to us.

We respond with shrugs and "Sure"s and go upstairs.

14

Rachel

I stand awkwardly in Nicole's room. The walls are covered with posters of bands and singers. Her desk is barely visible underneath piles of trendy brand-name clothes. Her CD player sits on her locker with heaps of CDs beside it.

Naomi, Jenny, Danielle and Nicole are all sitting on the bed, talking about school. And I'm just standing here. I look around at the posters to look occupied.

"Oh, God, we're completely leaving out Rachel," Nicole laughs. I like her already.

"Sorry, Rachel," Naomi says. "We just needed to fill Ms Rebel here in on school stuff."

"Ms Rebel," snorts Nicole. "You're just as bad as me, Naomi, except you can charm your way out of it."

"I know," Naomi smirks. "Hey, mind if I have a –"

"Don't even think about it," Nicole warns.

Naomi sighs.

"Hey, Rachel, sit down," Danielle invites, moving over on the bed to make room for me. I sit down.

"So how're things with Mark going?" Nicole asks Danielle.

"Oh! I forgot!" Danielle sounds really excited. She turns to me. "He said he'll dance with you at the disco!"

"Great!" I grin. At least I won't be standing around on my own for the first slow dance.

"And I'm dancing with Dónal!" Nicole sighs happily. He must be her boyfriend or something.

"How can we forget?" Naomi mutters.

"You can't!" Nicole grins. "Because he's absolutely gorgeous and he's going to dance with *me*."

"Note to self," I stage-whisper to Danielle. "Kidnap Dónal before the disco."

"Don't you dare!" Nicole shouts.

This is silly and fun and I love it. With these girls, I feel cool and popular and confident. I don't feel that with my friends at school. They're really nice and everything, but just being with these girls is somehow more exciting.

"Just remember," Jenny says, "if you can't be good, be careful . . ."

Nicole throws one of the pillows from the head of the bed at Jenny. Jenny catches it and tosses it back. Naomi grabs another and starts hitting me with it. I try to grab it away from her. Danielle takes another and starts attacking me with it. It's a full-fledged pillow-fight, or rather a pillow-bashing, and as there are only three pillows, it's not even a big one, but it's fun. I grab Danielle's pillow and start whacking her with it.

***

"We'd better go," Jenny says half an hour later. She crumples up an empty crisp packet. She gets up from the floor of Nicole's room and Danielle and Naomi follow suit. I suppose I'd better go as well. I'd feel too awkward with just me and Nicole. She's really friendly, but also, in a way, sort of intimidating. Anyway, I'm sure she doesn't want me around on my own.

"What about you, Rachel?" Nicole asks. "Do you have to get back home?"

I shrug. "It's not like there's anyone there waiting for me, no."

"So you want to stay?" she offers.

"Look who's getting all friendly," teases Danielle. I make a face at her.

"Don't you have to get back to school so that you're not late?" I say pointedly.

"Right," she replies.

We all go downstairs. Naomi, Jenny and Danielle leave. Nicole and I go into the sitting room and sit down on the couch.

"Great, an awkward silence," I say.

Nicole laughs. There's a silence for a while, then she says, "So, Danielle set you up with Mark?"

"Yeah. What's he like?"

"Oh, he's great, really friendly, really sensitive, a bit annoying though. And he's a great dancer, in case you were wondering! He probably won't try to meet you, but he might, you never know, but you don't need to worry, anyway, he's great at meeting!"

We laugh. Is this the time to mention I've never met a boy in my life and am useless at dancing? I think not.

"You *can* meet guys, right?" she asks. "I mean, like, you have before, haven't you?"

"Sure," I say, but she must know I'm lying. She looks at me closely.

"Hey, it's all right if you haven't, you know," she says gently. "I mean, considering that most of the guys our age are pricks anyway . . ."

I nod quietly. The feeling of coolness I've had since I got here has disappeared and I'm back to being quiet little me.

"So, anyway, Mark's really great," she continues. "He loves being all protective, as well, which is basically why he gave up on me and Danielle and Naomi. We're too tough for him!" She laughs. "He'll be thrilled if you show him your little quiet, teacher's pet side –" Nicole grins mischievously at me.

"Teacher's pet?" I exclaim. "Oh, you're dead!"

She squeals and leaps up and runs away. I chase her upstairs and then we start hitting each other and laughing.

15

Danielle

I call for Nicole on my way home, just to say hi. Rachel is still there.

"You're still here?" I say incredulously. Then to Nicole, "How did you put *up* with her for so long?"

Rachel makes a face at me and I smile sweetly back.

"She's way more fun than you," Nicole teases me.

"What did you do all afternoon – study?" I reply.

"I told her how to handle Mark," begins Nicole.

"Oh, that'd take all day," I interrupt.

"And then we watched *Titanic* for about the ten millionth time," Nicole continues.

I'm happy Rachel and Nicole are getting along now, but why do they have to be acting like they're the best of friends? I'm all for Rachel becoming friends with my friends, but why does she have to be a better friend than I am?

"Anyway," Nicole says, "my mum'll be home soon."

"So I'd better go," Rachel finishes. She steps down onto the driveway. "See you, Nicole."

"Yeah, bye," I add.

"Bye!" she calls after us as we walk home. It's weird, walking home with Rachel. We've been in different schools for the last two years, and even when we were in primary school we walked home with our different friends.

"Nicole's really nice, isn't she?" Rachel says as we turn onto our road.

I nod. "Yeah. So, did you talk about anything . . ."

"Yeah, she told me why she got suspended and how fed up she is with her mum and stuff like that."

I can't believe Nicole told Rachel all that stuff. This is serious. They spend one afternoon together and they're already really close friends. I'm not jealous, exactly. Okay, I am. I am so jealous of my little sister. I'm proud of her and I'm friends with her and I love her, she's my sister, but I envy her looks and brains and the way people seem to automatically like her.

At least she's in a different school, I reassure myself. As long as she's at her posh school and my friends and I are at the community school nothing too drastic can happen. I hope.

***

I yell over to Nicole the next morning. She's walking to school. Somehow, even though she has a heavy bag with loads of textbooks in it, she manages to be graceful. She tosses her blonde hair over her shoulder. I'm jealous of her hair. It's as long as Rachel's. Why do I have to be such a jealous cow? I ask myself.

Nicole doesn't hear me shout at first. I suppose anything other than an ear-splitting holler would seem like a whisper to her.

"YO! BLONDE BIMBO!" I scream as loudly as I can.

She carelessly runs across the road to join me outside the school and starts hitting me. I fight back.

"*Never* call me a blonde bimbo!" she exclaims.. She tries to pull at my hair but as it's so short it's pretty hard. I grab a handful of her silky fair hair and threaten to pull it.

"Okay, we're even," she screeches when I yank on her hair. We start to shake hands, and then she pulls hers away and starts chasing me into the school. I sprint in through the side door and pull it shut behind me. Nicole starts trying to open it and I pull at it to keep it shut. She wins and I start running down the corridor and crash into Mr Traynor. Nicole crashes into me and we fall over, pushing Mr Traynor on the floor as we do so.

I'm too horrified to say anything. Nicole looks at me in shock as we get up and help Mr Traynor up.

"Girls," he growls, "you *do* know what this means?"

I feel like crying.

***

He hauls us up to his office and then calls our friends over the intercom. Mr Traynor looks really annoyed. I'm so dead. If Mr Traynor doesn't murder me, then my friends will for getting them suspended as well and, if I'm lucky enough to survive that, my parents are going to go mad when they hear this. It's all my fault, and everyone's going to hate me.

71

Naomi arrives first. She doesn't even try to put on the innocent act and joins us gloomily. Tara comes in next. She's going to Australia tomorrow, so she might be let off. I wonder if we'll be sent home today or if he'll wait until next week.

Caitlin and Liz arrive together, and then Jenny and Grace file in. When we're all there, crammed into his office, he just stares at us for a few minutes.

"Due to the extremely unacceptable behaviour by two of you in the corridor this morning," he begins, "you will all be suspended."

Nicole looks as if she's about to protest, but he tells her not to even try with an icy look. "I warned you all this would happen," he continues. "Now, as Nicole and Danielle were the main, shall we say, perpetrators, they will each be suspended for today and next Monday. As for the rest of you, you will be suspended just for today. I'm going to phone your parents later on to inform them of this and they will also be receiving written notification."

I hear a choked sob and we all glance over. Grace is crying. I send her a sympathetic look. I wish so much none of us were having this stupid fight.

We all meekly file out of the office a few minutes later. We're all pretty depressed.

"I hate him so much!" Naomi exclaims. once we're well away from the office.

"I'm going to be so dead!" Nicole chokes out. Oh my God, she's actually crying. I'm stunned. "My mum kept on telling me not to get into trouble again like this, and look at me! I'm suspended for another two days!" She rubs her fists angrily at her eyes. "Oh, my God, the *disco!*" she suddenly screeches.

We all exchange horrified glances. "Oh, shit," Naomi mutters.

Jenny starts angrily chewing her nails.

"I have to get home, fake my mum's voice on the phone and somehow stop her from finding out about the suspension," Nicole says breathlessly. She's stopped crying. "I *have* to go to the disco! Come on, someone, come with me."

"I will," I volunteer. It's partly my fault. I should try to fix things as much as possible.

"So, what's everyone going to do today?" Caitlin asks in her gentle voice. "I can't go home; my mum's there." She looks around at everyone in the group, and I smile to myself. Mr Traynor is the common enemy now, no point fighting amongst ourselves. Caitlin's eyes meet mine and we smile tentatively at each other.

"What time will he phone our parents at?" wonders Jenny.

"Probably at lunch," guesses Naomi. "Is anyone's mum going to be home then?"

"Just mine," Caitlin says. "Everyone else's works. And I think my mum is going out for lunch today with her friends."

"So basically we have the whole day to ourselves before we get grounded forever?" asks Naomi.

We're at our lockers now, and get out our jackets and schoolbags. We continue walking down the corridor.

"Mm-hmm," murmurs Jenny.

"Well, we might as well have a good time before we get killed," Naomi says as if we're incredibly thick. "So . . . let's have some fun!"

"I'd prefer to go home and wallow in my misery," mutters Grace.

"Tough, babe," Naomi teases. "Come *on*, guys, let's *do* something!"

"All right," I agree. I feel like having fun. Considering that later I'll probably be given the 'Very Disappointed In You' lecture with lots of 'Why Can't You Be More Like Rachel?' added in, it's a *very* good idea.

"Well, I guess if he's not going to phone until later . . ." agrees Nicole.

Naomi cheers audibly. We hear a door opening down the hall, probably a teacher coming to reprimand us, and we sprint outside.

It's absolutely freezing outside. My skirt is rolled up about five times and my socks are rolled down to my ankles. It *looks* great, but it *feels* very cold. I pull my socks up to my knees.

"Nutgrove or the Square?" asks Liz. We're a couple of miles away from each of them.

"How 'bout we go to town?" suggests Naomi. "Come on, we can get the bus . . ."

We all cheer and high-five each other and agree to meet up at the bus stop in half an hour so that we have time to change and get money. I hurry home. Funny, even though I've just been suspended, I'm in an absolutely terrific mood.

16

Rachel

There are huge cheers as the announcement is made over the intercom. "As there is a problem with the electricity and none of the lights or radiators will work, all students will be allowed go home now." The rest of the announcement is drowned out as our entire class screams happily. We immediately leap up from our seats and gather up our books and dump them in our lockers.

I'm worried about how I'm going to get home. Mum is at work and it's too far to walk. Julie lends me the money to get the bus home and I'm very grateful. I arrive home to find Danielle about to leave.

"What're you doing here?" we say at the exact same time.

"The electricity's off in my school and they let us go home," I volunteer.

"I'm suspended," Danielle informs me. She doesn't sound devastated. "Nicole and I managed to knock our vice-principal on the ground this morning. We're suspended until Tuesday and the rest of our crowd are only suspended for one day. So we're going into town now to have some fun before we all get grounded."

"Oh," I say weakly. She's going to be in so much trouble.

***

The doorbell rings. Danielle answers it. It's Caitlin. "Come on," she says to Danielle. Then she sees me. "Rachel! What're you doing here?"

Danielle answers for me. I'm trying to figure out how Caitlin has suddenly forgiven Danielle.

"Well, are you going to come with us then?" Caitlin asks. "Hurry up and get changed, will you?"

I run upstairs and tear my uniform off. I pull on my navy jeans and borrow Danielle's white and navy Ellesse jacket, slip on my runners, grab my wallet and keys, and jump downstairs two minutes later, ready to go.

"You look great!" exclaims Caitlin. We leave the house and close the front door behind us. The old woman who lives across the road looks out the window, sees us, and purses her lips disapprovingly. She probably thinks we're mitching or something.

We run down to the bus stop, the one at the other end of our estate. Naomi and Jenny are standing there. Naomi looks particularly cool and sophisticated, dangling a cigarette from her fingers.

"After all they tell us in SAPP and science and home ec about smoking being bad for you, you still do it," Caitlin sighs. She sounds like she's said this a hundred times before with no result.

"The warnings are right on the packet," adds Danielle. "Come on. Put it out."

"I'm under stress," Naomi replies sweetly. "I'll just have this one before Nicole gets here and kills me."

"And she *will* kill you, you know," Tara adds, joining us. Is it Tara? Yeah, I think so. "Hiya, Rachel. Didn't think you were the type to go on the hop."

"I'm not," I reply. "They closed the school because the lights and heating were off."

"You lucky bitch!" she responds. "Yesterday *and* today off school? God, I picked the wrong school to go to, that's for sure."

"Definitely," Jenny agrees.

I can see three girls approaching us. Liz, Grace and Nicole quicken their pace and join us. After explanations for my presence, we wait impatiently for the bus. Nicole and I start fighting – messing, of course. It's great. My friends at school are never like this. Compared to these girls, they're boring and dull. I know I shouldn't think that way about my loyal friends, but Danielle's friends seem to be much more fun than my friends. Except for Michelle, but I don't see her that often.

The bus takes ages to come. I suppose seeing as it's the middle of the day it's not exactly in a big rush. The bus driver shoots us suspicious looks as we board. We buy our tickets and hurry up to the top of the bus, where we squash into the seats at the front and look down. There aren't a lot of cars on the roads now; I suppose everyone is already in work.

When we finally reach town we're not sure which stop to get off at and have a big argument over it. We're just messing, of course – I don't think these girls take anything seriously. I like that. My friends are all so serious, worrying about exams and not being able to take a joke.

These days the shops are usually packed with Christmas shoppers, but as it's only eleven in the morning on a weekday the shops are relatively empty. We debate over which shop to go to first and finally agree on HMV. We look through the CDs and cassettes and posters and videos while the shop assistants are watching our every move. If it wasn't so insulting I'd laugh. It reminds me of how in first year home economics we were discussing stereotypical roles and we had to give three examples of this. One of mine was, *All teenagers are shoplifters*. On the very rare occasions that my friends and I have gone shopping together, the shop assistants are always keeping an eye on us, as if we're going to steal something.

"I feel like I should nick a CD just to keep them happy," Nicole murmurs in my ear, and I try to suppress a giggle.

Caitlin buys the latest Five single and we leave. Our next stop is Clerys, where we head straight for Miss Selfridge. We look at all the clothes. I check my wallet. I have thirty pounds with me and there is a gorgeous zip-up cardigan top thing that I absolutely love that is only twelve pounds. The others admire it and encourage me to buy it. I find it in my size and buy it.

We examine every little item of jewellery in the whole of Dublin city. It seems every jewellery counter we pass at the department stores, every jewellery shop, is scrutinised. Danielle falls in love with a pair of dangly sterling silver heart earrings and gives me some not-so-subtle hints that she would like those for Christmas.

"They're gorgeous, Rachel, aren't they? I love them, but they're eight quid and I can't afford them if I'm going to get you and Mum and Dad your Christmas presents . . . God, I wish someone would get those for me for Christmas, they're just the sort of thing I would want someone, say my darling sister, to give me . . ."

That's my sister, all right. I buy the earrings and now have ten pounds left. We all decide to go to McDonald's and spend about an hour there at a four-person table which nine of us are squeezed around, nibbling at chips and talking and laughing. Between us we only buy about five meals, as some of them are nearly broke or aren't hungry or whatever, but they still end up eating something, and when we're just sitting there taking tiny sips of Coke about every five minutes, the staff are shooting us don't-you-think-it's-about-time-you-left? looks, but we don't care.

It's fun, it's friendly, it's cool, and I love it.

17

Danielle

Rachel and I make sure to be home by four. She phoned Mum from town telling her about her school being closed early, but no mention was made of the trip into town, or the suspension. Mum arrives home just as the phone rings. It has to be Mr Traynor. I leap for it, thinking I'll tell him it's a wrong number or just hang up or fake her voice or something, but Mum gets there first. I hurry up to my room.

A few minutes later I hear her yell, "DANIELLE!"

I guess he told her. I jump down the stairs and into the sitting room, where my mother is standing, looking extremely pissed off.

"What is the meaning of this, young lady?" she begins. "I thought you were going to stay out of trouble, and now I find out you're *suspended*? Along with *seven* of your friends? I hope you have an explanation, Danielle."

"He's being totally unfair. It was only me and Nicole that

got into trouble, but he suspended the whole lot of us. That wasn't fair. He warned us he was going to suspend all of us if any of us got into trouble before Christmas, and Mum, he's being really mean about that, because only half of us ever get into trouble at all, and when Nicole told him that, he suspended her. Now isn't *that* unfair?"

"I don't care whether you think it's unfair or not, Danielle. The rules are there for a reason and it's not up to you to question those in authority."

Even if those in authority are totally screwed up? I feel like asking, but don't.

"You're grounded for the weekend, and any more cheek from you and you won't be going to the Christmas disco. Is that clear? The only reason I'm letting you go after this is because I don't want Rachel to be there by herself, understood? Now, any more bad behaviour from you and you'll be asking me to punish you *and* your sister."

"Yeah, Mum," I mutter and retreat to my room. What a bitch, I think, and Rachel echoes my sentiments exactly when she hears about it.

"It could have been worse, though," she said. "You're only grounded for the weekend! You still get to watch TV, use the phone, go on the Internet, get your pocket money, and you can still go the disco! I bet none of your friends will get off so lightly."

She's right, I realise. I wonder if any of my friends will end up going to the disco. Then I wonder how many of them that will be grounded will try to sneak out. Jenny will if Naomi pushes her, and Nicole definitely will. Liz will probably check her horoscope to see if it tells her "Doom will fall upon you if you rebel against the wishes of the people you care about" or if it says "If you force yourself to do that thing, you will be successful; if not, you will be miserable." Liz is a great believer in astrology.

Suddenly the lights go off. I scream in surprise. It's already dark outside, and I can't see anything. There's been a power cut, I realise. Today seems to be a day for electricity problems, first with Rachel's school and now this. I wonder if they're connected.

"Danielle?" Rachel's voice sounds shaky and scared.

"Yeah?" I respond. "Are you okay?"

"Yeah," she answers in a wobbly voice. I feel like protecting her, for some reason, and go over to her and put my arms around her. She hugs me back. She's trembling, I realise.

"Why're you scared?" I ask her gently. "You can't be scared of the dark, can you?"

"I'm not," she says, not sounding convinced at all.

"Yeah, you are," I say quietly.

"I'm not a little kid any more."

"Just 'cause you're scared of something doesn't mean you're a little kid. I'm still scared of spiders, for God's sake."

We sit down on the bed. Mum calls up to us. "Girls, are you okay?"

"Yeah, we're fine!" I shout back.

I feel a tickling sensation at the base of my neck and realise it's moving. It feels like a spider. Oh no. "Get it off me!" I shriek.

Rachel bursts into laughter and removes her hand from my neck.

"Very funny," I snap and we start hitting each other.

***

The power still isn't back half an hour later. It reminds me of Christmas Eve a few years ago, when all the power went off, and I never got to see the end of *Look Who's Talking Now*. I got very huffy.

Dad is home. Candles have been lit and torches are turned on. The sitting room is relatively well lit, and even though Dad is saying the light is too poor to be reading in, Rachel and I are curled up at opposite ends of the couch and reading. She is in the middle of *Angela's Ashes* by Frank McCourt and I'm finishing *She's The One* by Cathy Kelly.

"Didn't think you knew *how* to read anything besides *Sugar*," teases Rachel, momentarily putting her book down.

I stick my tongue out at her. She has a point, though. I hardly ever read anything, apart from magazines, but Cathy Kelly's books are really good. So are Maeve Binchy's, but they're just not as *fun* to read. I read the last page of *She's The One* and then close it, sighing. I wish the power was back on. I'm missing *Home and Away*.

The power comes back on and I get to see the closing scene of *Home and Away*. I turn on Sky One and we watch *The Simpsons* together, me and Rachel.

"Power cuts make people bond," Rachel says when the ads come on. Sky One always have such long ad breaks, it really gets on my nerves.

"Oh, God, NO!" I pretend to be horrified. "It can't be –"
Rachel nods in mock sadness. "I hate to tell you this, but
we've-we've-we've –" she stammers dramatically.

"What is it?" I ask, mock-fearfully.

"We've bonded!"

I pretend to shoot myself. Rachel laughs and stretches
out on the couch.

18

Rachel

The weekend is dull and boring. On Sunday evening Danielle gets an e-mail from Tara in Australia, describing her flight and the car journey. That's basically the high point of my weekend, apart from maybe sitting slumped in front of the TV watching endless *Friends* videos with Danielle. Not forgetting hearing Mum nagging me, asking 'Now shouldn't you be studying for your Christmas exams?' and so on.

Studying used to be tolerable, I even found it interesting sometimes, if it was home ec or history or English, but now it's incredibly boring. I tell Danielle this and she says, "Finally, my sister is normal!"

Back in school on Monday, with thirteen days to go until Christmas – I'm getting just like Danielle and Lauren – I find my friends extremely uninteresting. They talk – just *talk*, not whisper or giggle or laugh or shriek, just talk – about homework and the Christmas exams. Julie starts describing her Christmas outfit, and I listen eagerly to this interesting piece of information. Then Siobhán starts complaining that she can never get gorgeous clothes that fit as they're always too big for her, and we start discussing which shops are the best to buy clothes in, and I start enjoying myself. These, I am sure, are the sorts of things Danielle and her friends are always talking about, not mundane things like homework and exams, but clothes and music and boys.

All my homework is neatly done in my bag. I spent ages doing it on Wednesday night, when I got most of it. Neat and organised, that's me, I think gloomily. I don't want to be neat and organised all the time.

We are given English homework to do for tomorrow and I start on it immediately, rushing it so that I don't need to do it tonight. So what if I haven't written out a million rough drafts or thought everything through a hundred times? No one ever said I had to be Ms Absolutely Brilliant all the time, did they? Certainly my mother expects me to be, but maybe if I get lower marks she'll appreciate it more when I do really well. I'm sure there's some deep psychological reason why suddenly I don't care if I'm not Miss 100% the entire time, but I suppose the short version is that Danielle and her friends have shown me that there are plenty of things in life other than school, and most of them are much more fun, too.

***

At lunch, when we're all hanging around the classroom, I describe to Siobhán, Julie and Lauren my day in town with Danielle and her friends. "And then we just sat around in

McDonald's for ages," I say. "The people who work there looked fed up with us."

"Must've been nice," Siobhán says wistfully. "I spent the whole day watching TV."

"Same here," sighed Julie.

"I went to Nutgrove and did my Christmas shopping," Lauren volunteers.

"I did mine already," I say.

"You would," mutters Lauren.

"What's *that* supposed to mean?" I ask her icily, staring her right in the eye. I'm fed up with her being a bitch towards me. Would Danielle or Naomi or Nicole put up with this? No, and neither will I.

"Nothing," she says innocently.

"Lauren, you've been making little bitchy remarks for ages now. I'm getting pretty fed up with it. If you want to say something, then just say it. If you don't like me, fine, because right now I don't like you that much either." I fold my arms and keep my eyes glued to hers.

"Oh, no, Little Miss Perfect doesn't like me. How will I cope?" she sneers.

"Probably bore us all to death talking about that moron Carl," I reply sweetly.

Lauren sees she's losing the battle, and she storms off, tossing a "Bitch!" at me over her shoulder. Once she's out of the classroom, Julie, Siobhán and I cheer.

"Way to go, Rache!" Siobhán exclaims.

I stand up and take mock bows. "Thank you, thank you, cash contributions only, please."

"I never thought you could speak up like that," Julie says admiringly. "I mean, you're always so quiet."

"Must be Danielle's influence," I say. "Next thing you know I'll be getting you all suspended."

"I can't wait," Siobhán says dryly.

***

After lunch we have the maths test that Ms Lynch told us would be on Friday. Seeing as we missed maths then, she springs it on us on Monday. Amid complaints and groans, she hands out the test papers.

I haven't studied. In fact, I can barely remember what we did in class with these sums. I look down at the questions and realise that I've forgotten how to do them. I do my best, but when I've handed up the test I'm pretty sure I haven't got 100%. In fact, I'm doubtful as to whether I've passed or not. I voice these concerns to Julie, but she thinks I've done brilliantly as usual and that I'm just fishing for compliments. I wish that were true.

I wonder how everyone will react if I fail this Maths test. Will my friends be shocked? Will Mum give out to me? And do I even care whether I pass or not? No. I don't.

19

Danielle

Mum works in a pharmacy and is gone by the time I'm dressed on Monday morning. Dad, of course, has been gone since seven-thirty, and I wander around the empty house, bored.

Nicole comes over later on in the morning. I show her the e-mail I got from Tara yesterday, as Nicole doesn't have e-mail on her computer, and then we sit around the house, bored. Do I prefer being bored alone or bored with a friend, I wonder. Being suspended – and grounded – is definitely not fun. Admittedly Friday was, but now all our money is gone and most of our friends are back at school, except for Tara, who is no doubt working on her tan on the beach right now while we're stuck in freezing cold Ireland.

I tell Nicole about how I'm allowed go to the disco because of Rachel. "I'm not sure it's going to be that great, though," I sigh. "I mean, I wanted it to be all of us from school and Rachel, but since most of our friends probably won't be allowed go . . . it's going to be crap."

"I know," she agrees, tossing her hair. It's in a long plait today. "I'm allowed to go – my next-door neighbour pretended to be my mum on the phone and I faked her signature. So Mum doesn't know I'm suspended."

We start discussing the disco and then Nicole brings up the topic of Mark and Rachel.

"So what about Rachel? I mean, have you told Mark to go easy on her and not start groping her right away?"

"Mark's not like that," I defend him. "He's really sweet and sensitive . . . he wouldn't do that to her. That's just the type of person he is."

"Sounds like someone fancies someone," she teases.

"Mark? God, why does everyone think that? We're just friends. I know that and he knows that."

"He's mad about you! The only reason he let himself get set up with Rachel is because he'd do anything you ask him to!"

"That is *so* not true. He got set up with her because everyone was saying nice stuff about Rachel. He'll love her. He'll love being Mr Protective. Which, if you remember, is why Mark and I could never go together. He always needs to be the strong macho man."

"Macho, macho man," Nicole starts singing.

"Shut up, you crow," I tease her. Actually, she's a great singer.

"*Moi?* I'm a brilliant singer. You, on the other hand . . ."

I grab a cushion from the armchair and whack her on the head with it. She sticks her tongue out at me.

"Very mature," I say sarcastically.

"I'm *very* mature," she protests. She sits straight in the

chair and places her hands on her knees. She puts a dignified expression on her face.

"Looks can be deceiving," I mutter.

***

We go the newsagents' around the corner around lunchtime. The crowd from our school with lunch passes are coming down the road and we hurry in before the crowd comes in. We buy our sweets and leave. The girl at the counter looks at us suspiciously in our Adidas gear and I know she thinks we're on the hop. Well, so what?

Then we walk up to the school to see our friends. They're supposed to be at sports, but Naomi and Jenny haven't bothered and we see them coming out of the building. We yell over to them. Actually Nicole yells at the top of her voice and I just call over to them.

They hurry towards us and we exchange hugs as if we've been separated forever. "Anything interesting happen today?" I ask as the four of us walk down towards the estates.

"Oh, Liz was sent home sick," Jenny volunteers. "She went up to Mr Traynor when we had him for Irish and puked all over his shoes."

Nicole explodes in laughter.

"Calm *down*," I say sweetly. She makes a face at me.

"So he hates all of us even more now," continues Jenny cheerfully. "Loads of people are out today. It's that bug that's going around. We had a free science class because the teacher was out."

"You okay, Naomi?" Nicole asks her.

I look over at Naomi. She's being unusually quiet. Either she's sulking or else something's wrong. She looks kind of pale, too.

"I feel sick," she volunteers quietly.

"Still?" Jenny asks. "Maybe you should go home and not come back for the afternoon."

"Yeah, I think I will," Naomi says.

Mark and Robbie join us and start walking along with us. "Hi, Danielle," Mark says. "Oh, yeah, hi, everyone else." He's messing.

"Uh . . . Danielle . . ." Robbie stammers, "did you think about what I asked you?"

"Just one admirer after the other," teases Jenny.

"You mean that little question that caused me and my friends to have that huge fight?" I say sweetly.

He winces. "Sorry."

"What's wrong with Caitlin, anyway?" I ask him bluntly.

"She's . . . oh, I don't know, a real Miss Perfect at everything. She makes me feel about two inches tall."

"Centimetres," Mark corrects him and grins at me. I smile back.

"Whatever," Robbie says.

"But she really likes you!" I say.

We reach the estate where Naomi and Robbie live and they go in. Mark walks along with us three girls, casually sliding his arm around my shoulder. I remove it.

"Is your sister as much of a tease?" he asks.

"Rachel?" I snort. "She's very prim and proper – you might want to rethink your usual strategy."

"Which would be what, exactly?" he asks.

Nicole and I exchange looks. "First you pretend to be really nice," I say sweetly.

"Then you meet the poor, defenceless girl," Nicole continues.

"Then you start feeling her," I add.

"Me? You make me sound like a horrible person!" he protests.

"Oh, we're only joking," I reassure him.

"So you *will* be the mother of my children?" he asks in mock hope.

"Dream on," I answer. He goes into his house, and I gaze after him. He's a really great guy. Perfect for Rachel, I think. Then suddenly it hits me. Or maybe, perfect for *me*?

20

Rachel

We get our maths tests back that afternoon from Ms Lynch.

"These test scores were *appalling*!" she declares, handing out the copies. I cross my fingers as I open mine. Fifty-eight. I never thought I'd be so happy about getting a C.

"What'd you get?" Siobhán asks.

"Fifty-eight. What about you?"

"Sixty-two," she replies. "Hey, I actually did better than you!"

Julie whispers back to us. We give her our scores and it turns out she got sixty-five. It seems no one's done really well on this test.

"I mean," Ms Lynch continues, "none of you seem to understand these sums. The highest score was, I think . . ." – she consults her notebook – "eighty-two. I would expect more from this class." She seems to be looking straight at me and I gaze innocently back. I've never received lower than an A before in my entire life. My academic record is not going to suffer because of one C.

***

Collecting me after school, Mum asks about the maths test. I thought she would have forgotten about it.

"I passed," I say neutrally.

"With an A, I hope," she mutters.

I feel angry with her. Nothing is good enough for her except top marks.

"Actually, a C," I snap.

"What? Did you study for it? Did you try hard enough?"

Now she's insinuating I didn't try hard enough. I hate her.

"No, I didn't study," I reply tartly. "There are more things to life than studying, you know."

"You sound just like your sister," she groans.

"Good."

The rest of the journey home is spent in silence. Danielle is in the sitting-room watching the cartoons on *Nickelodeon*. I flop down beside her.

"Do your homework first, Rachel," Mum reminds me.

"Don't have any," I reply. I did it at lunchtime.

"The disco's in four days," Danielle says. "And listen to this. There's a bug going round our school, and Liz has it and Naomi probably does as well. So they probably won't be able to go. Then I rang Jenny a couple of minutes ago, and it turns out her mum isn't letting her go, *and* Caitlin and Grace are grounded as well."

"It's not going to be any fun if most of them aren't there," I agree. "So it's just us two and Nicole?"

"Mm-hmm, unless we can convince Jenny to sneak out, which won't be that hard, and unless Naomi or Liz get better."

"I hope they do." We settle back for a while, and then I say, "So, I got my maths test back today."

"Don't tell me. 100%."

"How about 58%?" I ask.

"What? My brilliant brainy sister got 58%?" She does an imitation of Janice from *Friends* and says "Oh my *Gawd*" in a New York accent.

"It's going to wreck my whole life," I joke. "Now I can never become a maths teacher."

"Your whole life-plan down the drain," Danielle agrees in mock-seriousness.

***

Julie rings me that night. She asks me about the homework and what I got for the answers to the geography questions. It's very boring. Why can't she phone with some gossip about one of the girls in our class or to talk about anything other than school?

I can't believe these thoughts are coming from me. I've always been known as the brain of the class, and now I'm starting to hate school?

I voice these concerns to Danielle and she responds with, "You hate school, that's normal. But you can still be the brain of the class if you hate school."

Personally I don't see how, but I suppose I'll have to try. I always feel I have to do really well in school, first of all to please my parents, second of all because I was moved up a year and feel like I constantly have to prove I deserved it. But pleasing my parents doesn't seem so important any more, and it's ridiculous trying to be the top of the class all the time.

"Earth to Rachel!" Danielle waves a hand in front of my eyes. "Anyone in there?"

"Yeah, I'm here."

"Good. *Friends* is going to be on in a couple of minutes on Network 2." She changes the channel and a white 2 appears in the corner of the screen before disappearing.

We assume comfortable positions on the couch and settle back to enjoy thirty minutes of hilarity, comedy, and Matthew Perry. Could life *be* any better?

21

Danielle

Back to school on Tuesday just in time for the start of the Christmas exams. Naomi arrives in looking pale and weak but determined to do the exams. Caitlin is almost in tears with nervousness, the way she is before all the major exams. I dread to think what she'll be like before the Junior Cert. She starts biting her nails. By the time our first exam starts her fingernails will be reduced to nothing.

"I'm knackered," I yawn. "I stayed up until eleven-thirty last night studying."

"Poor Danielle," Mark says. A whole group of us are sitting on the desks in a classroom before school starts – me, Caitlin, Naomi, Mark, Darragh, Seán.

"Would you like me to rearrange your face?" I ask him sweetly.

Nicole sticks her head around the door. "Assembly!" she reminds us. We jump off the desks and race down to the hall. I totally forgot.

Mr Traynor is already there and he frowns at the seven of us as we file in. He doesn't give us black marks, though, which is at least something to be grateful for. We sit down on one of the unoccupied benches.

"I am very disturbed with the behaviour of the second-years," Mr Traynor says. "Last week I was forced to suspend eight girls from second year."

Nicole, Naomi and I exchange grins. Everyone turns to look at us. They've all heard about how unfair Mr Traynor was.

"I do not like suspending pupils," he continues.

Yeah, right, I think. Suspending eight of us when what he should have done was give Nicole and me detention – no, of course he doesn't *like* suspending pupils.

"But sometimes it is necessary in order to make pupils realise how badly they have behaved. I do not want to have to give out any more black marks, or detentions, or suspensions, but I will if necessary. I hope you won't make it necessary." He seems to be looking over at me and my friends.

"Now, your Christmas exams start today, I believe you have –"

"English and maths," we all chorus.

"English and maths," he repeats. "Remember, take your time, follow the instructions, and do your best. You can go now."

Naomi looks really wrecked, I realise as we go back to class. She should be at home. Okay, so she'd miss the exam, but she won't be able to do well on it today if she's sick.

We have our first class and then have to go to the exam

hall on the top floor for our maths exam. Caitlin bursts into tears. Exams really stress her out – her parents put pressure on her.

"What's wrong?" Robbie asks her gently.

Yes! I say to myself. He's talking to her, he's being Mr Sensitive. Great.

"Just . . . I don't know," she stammers. "I always get like this before exams."

"But you've nothing to worry about," he says. "You know you'll do well on the exams. You always do." He smiles at her and Caitlin dries her eyes. We enter the exam hall and sit down at the desks and wait for our tests to be given out.

***

"That was awful," groans Adam an hour later as we go back to class.

"Actually, I thought it was really easy," says Caitlin.

"It was easier than I thought it'd be," I volunteer.

"I missed about half the questions," says Robbie.

"Do you think they put you in the Higher or Normal Maths class based *just* on this test?" asks Grace worriedly. "Because I've done really well in maths since the start of last year but I know I did really crap on that exam."

All of the second-years are going to get put into the different ability maths classes after Christmas. That's why this particular maths exam was so important. And why I actually bothered studying.

"You'll get into Higher Level maths, Grace, don't worry," says Dónal.

"And you'll have to do more work," Jenny points out. "I know I'll be in the lower class. I'm useless at maths and anyway the teacher hates me."

We arrive back in our class five minutes before break is due to begin. Our teacher hasn't come, so I suppose she won't come at all now. I start munching on a bar of chocolate.

"Hi," Mark says, sliding into the empty chair beside me. Tara's usual place.

"Hi," I answer.

"So, how d'you think you did on the exam?" he asked.

"All right. How 'bout you?"

"I think I got either a low A or a high B," he says.

"Brainbox," I laugh. "That's why you and Rachel are obviously made for each other. You could recite French verbs together. You know, before you start groping her."

"I do not grope!" he protests.

"Sure you do. Remember at the disco a couple of weeks ago when you danced with me?"

"I've grown up since then?" he tries.

I laugh. "You're great."

"Thanks, Danielle. You have nice . . ." he trails off suggestively and grins mischievously. I hit him on the head.

"Nice handwriting?"

"Give it up, Mark."

"Anything for you, my darling."

"Why don't you take anything seriously?" I ask him in a serious tone and look at him closely. He blushes under my scrutiny.

"You're blushing," I say delightedly. He looks so cute.

"I am not!" he protested.

"It makes you look cute," I tell him.

"Great. I'm like a little hamster or something now, am I?"

"Don't worry. You're also gorgeous," I say bluntly.

"I get that a lot," he kids.

"I'm going to strangle you some day," I say sweetly. I get up and go to my locker to get my books out.

Mark's a really great guy, I think. Funny and smart and sensitive and . . . oh, God, *such* a babe.

But I like him just as a friend, I tell myself firmly. And I've set him up with my sister who is perfect for him.

Just as a friend, I repeat. Just as a friend.

22

Rachel

I look at my science test in despair. I hate science. I'm good at it if I try really hard, but lately I haven't been bothering.

I think of Danielle. Lucky her, with only her English and maths Christmas exams today. If I had those I'd be ecstatic. But no, I have to get three exams today, with two of my worst subjects. We've already had history, which was easy, and after this there's geography, which I hate.

I answer as many questions as possible and then try to guess my score. I think I got nearly all of the biology questions right, then just over half of the physics. Seeing as there was more biology than anything else, I'm guessing that will be about 40% of my actual score, and that the physics will be about 15%. At least I know I passed. And I don't even want to *think* about the chemistry.

***

Danielle and I exchange exam horror stories throughout the week. By Friday, we're both totally fed up with exams. On

Monday she has her history and geography exams and I have my home ec and French exams.

Friday night is greatly anticipated and when it arrives we're both very happy. Danielle and I have decided I will wear the top I got at Miss Selfridge with black tights and her denim miniskirt. She is wearing black hipsters with a gorgeous low-cut purple top.

I plait my hair and then we start doing our make-up. At least, Danielle starts delicately applying about a hundred liquids and powers and creams to her face and I tentatively put on some green eyeshadow.

When we're ready, we walk down to the community centre. I'm glad Danielle's with me. I'd hate to have to walk in there by myself. We walk in the door and go down the corridor. When we go into the disco, after paying at the door, it's crowded and music is blaring. We join Nicole and Caitlin.

"I thought you were supposed to be grounded!" Danielle has to scream at Caitlin so that she can be heard over the music.

"Robbie is going to dance with me!" Caitlin yells back. "Did you think I was going to miss THAT?"

"You're so bold, Caitlin," I tease her.

"I know, I know," she grins.

"Hi!" I hear a boy yell, and we all turn around. He's gorgeous, with dark brown hair and amazing blue eyes and a mischievous look on his face. And he's just the right height – just a tiny bit taller than me.

Oh please let this be Mark, I find myself wishing.

"Hi, Mark!" Nicole hollers at him.

It's Mark, he's Mark, he's absolutely gorgeous and I'm going to have to dance with him and I won't have a clue what to do or say or anything.

"Rachel?" he asks me.

I nod. I don't feel capable of screaming at the top of my lungs.

"It's too loud in here. I'll talk to you outside," he tells me, and I follow him, weaving through the crowds until we're out in the corridor.

"So . . . you're Rachel," he says.

"Don't get *too* enthusiastic," I say sweetly.

"Sorry . . . it's just that when Danielle said she was bringing her little brainbox sister I didn't imagine someone like you."

"I choose to take that as a compliment."

"It was." He winks at me. I blush.

"Come on, let's go back inside," he continues, and we go back in. The first slow song begins to play and I panic. What do I do?

The crowd seems to thin out on the dance floor now, more people go to the edges and watch the people who are slow-dancing. We put our arms around each other, a bit awkwardly at first, and then we smile at each other and get it right, and start slowly shuffling around. Once the arms are sorted out, there's really nothing much else to do.

"I wonder what would happen if I tried to kiss you," he murmurs into my ear.

"You'd probably end up bashing your nose into my ear or something," I whisper back and we both laugh.

Secretly I'm worried. What if he does try to kiss me? I'm not sure whether I want him to or not.

My head is on his shoulder. We both move back slightly at exactly the same time. I look into his eyes and then blush and look down.

Then suddenly his lips are meeting mine and I just somehow know what to do, and I love this and I'm crazy about Mark and I never want this song to end.

23

Danielle

Nicole and I are leaning against the wall watching the slow-dancing. Dónal hasn't shown up yet.

We watch Caitlin with Robbie and then Nicole says, "So, do you think Mark likes Rachel?"

"I don't know," I answer. "But she likes him, definitely." I'm not exactly sure how I feel about this whole thing and I really don't want to think about it.

"I wonder what Rachel'll do if Mark tries anything," I say. Nicole isn't listening. She's staring intently at a couple on the dance floor who are meeting each other. Actually, they look like they're doing a bit more than that. It looks extremely passionate and – oh, my God. I don't believe this! It's Mark and Rachel! My little baby sister certainly looks like she knows what she's doing.

"She told me she'd never met anyone," Nicole informs me.

"She hasn't."

"Guess she's making up for lost time," she says.

The slow song ends and Rachel and Mark cling to each other for a little bit longer before releasing each other and joining us.

"Hi," Rachel says. Her face is red and hot and wisps of hair have escaped from her plait. It's not fair. She looks gorgeous.

"Mark, uh . . . was that your idea of not groping?" Nicole wants to know.

He smirks. "You'll never know."

"Thank God," she replies.

Mark and Rachel look at each at the same time, blush and then smile. I'm not sure whether I'm happy they like each other or whether I'm upset because I like Mark. At least I think I do. I'm not sure. Oh, give it up, Danielle, I tell myself, you're absolutely mad about him. Just try to get through tonight without doing anything stupid.

Dónal arrives and joins us.

"About time," mutters Nicole.

"What'd I miss?" he asks.

"Just Mark getting off with Rachel," Nicole says lightly. "Come on, let's go and dance." She practically drags him away.

I'm left with Mark and Rachel. Mark runs his hand through his hair. "Want to go dance again?" he asks her.

"Sure," she nods and they move out into the middle of the floor. She's a good dancer, actually.

Caitlin and Robbie are dancing together as well. I'm left on my own. Caitlin, Robbie, Mark, Rachel, Dónal and

Nicole are in a group together, showing off. They look like they're having loads of fun, and I feel hot tears forming in my eyes. I wish Rachel wasn't here. I usually dance with Mark at the discos, just messing around, of course, and now he's with Rachel there's no room for me in the group.

"Are you all right?" a girl from my class, Ann, asks me as she passes by.

I force myself to grin. "Yeah, why wouldn't I be?" I make her feel a bit silly for asking, I can tell, and she hurries off, embarrassed.

I look over at my friends again and then turn away and begin pushing my way through the crowd out of the disco, keeping my head down so that no one can see I'm crying. I lean against the hard, cool wall once I'm outside. I'm almost expecting one of my friends to hurry out and see if I'm okay, but apparently no one's noticed. No one cares, I think miserably. I go into the girls' bathroom and dry my eyes, dabbing at them with a wet tissue. Then I look coolly at my reflection in the mirror. "No one cares about me. So what?" I say fiercely. I toss the tissue into the bin and stride out and go back into the disco.

"Danielle!" Nicole yells to me when I come back in. I scan the crowd for her. There's a whole group from our class now and I push my way over to them.

"Hi!" I say breezily.

"Gorgeous outfit, Danielle," says Samantha. Then she goes over to talk to Rachel. They used to be good friends in primary school, I remember.

We're having a great time dancing until another slow

song comes on. Yes, another one. They seem to be coming much more frequently than usual, or maybe I'm just being paranoid. The couples split off from the others and the rest of us edge off.

Mark and Rachel are glued together again. One dance, I think. I set them up for one dance. Not two. Not a lifetime's worth. I try to avoid looking at them but my eyes are forced to look over at them. He's meeting her again. And again. I bite fiercely into my lip and go over to Eric and Adam who are drinking Coke in the corner. Adam smiles at me but Eric is too busy staring intently at someone in the middle of the hall.

"Hiya," I say. I get a can from the vending machine and tentatively open it. Coke fizzes out of the top and I delicately lick it off and begin to sip.

"You want to dance the next slow dance with me?" Adam asks, just as I hoped.

I shrug. "Sure."

"See you then," he says.

Smiling with satisfaction I saunter off. Adam's not Mark but at least now I'll have someone to dance with. And maybe it'll take my mind off Mark.

24

Rachel

"I'll see ya sometime over the weekend, all right?" Mark says.

"Sure, whatever," I smile at him.

"Well, I have to go now. Bye."

"Bye," I say. I watch him as he walks off. "Wow," I sigh.

"I've never seen him fancying any girl so much," Nicole comments. Danielle, Nicole, and I are waiting outside the community centre for her mum to pick us up. It's eleven-thirty, too late to walk home even if there are three of us and it's just down the road.

"Except maybe you, of course," Nicole says to Danielle. "But he's definitely getting over you now. I bet you're happy."

Danielle doesn't look happy. She looks pretty miserable, actually. I wonder why. She looked as if she was having a great time all night.

"Yeah," she says in a flat tone.

"You okay?" Nicole asks her, putting an arm around her.

"Yeah, I'm fine," she replies.

Nicole's mum arrives. She seems nice enough. It's hard to believe she's the same person who Nicole hates so much. She drops me and Danielle off at our house.

"So . . . Mark's really great, isn't he?" I sigh.

"Yeah," Danielle says unenthusiastically.

I'm in such a great mood. I really like Mark. And I think he really likes me, otherwise he wouldn't have danced all the slow dances with me, right? I bounce up the driveway and ring the doorbell happily. Danielle trudges along behind me.

***

Danielle and I run into Mark outside the supermarket on Saturday. Mum sent us to get some messages.

"Hi," we all greet each other. Then Danielle storms off into the supermarket.

"What's her problem?" I mutter.

Mark shrugs. "She's probably just annoyed about something else. She'll get over it."

I nod. "So . . . how's it going?"

"All right. Well, I have to get home. See ya, Rache."

"See ya," I echo and follow Danielle into the supermarket.

"What is *up* with you?" I ask Danielle when I find her shoving baguettes into a paper bag.

"Nothing," she sighs. "Absolutely nothing." If I didn't know my sister so well, I'd swear she was about to cry.

"Fine," I say. But I know there's something wrong. She's been acting weird ever since the disco and she refuses to tell me why or even admit it.

While we're walking home, I ask her again, "Come on, Danielle. What's wrong?"

"I *told* you, nothing. Just leave me alone, okay?" she snaps and storms off down the road.

***

Danielle and I don't talk to each other for the rest of the weekend. Our parents notice but don't say anything; we hardly ever talk to each other anyway. I'm pretty upset about this, though, because I wanted to stay friends with Danielle.

I try to figure out why she's annoyed with me, and I can't think of anything. On Sunday night I can't get to sleep, thinking about it. At about one o' clock I finally get up and wander around the house. It's weird at night, full of shadows and darkness, and I admit I'm a little bit scared. I slip into Danielle's room and expect to see her sleeping peacefully. Instead, when I come in she turns over and pulls the duvet over her head. I can hear muffled sobs.

"Are you okay?" I ask her gently. "Come on, just tell me what's wrong."

"Get lost," she mutters, sticking her head out, revealing a tear-stained face.

I sit down on the bed. "Why were you crying?"

"None of your fucking business, all right? Just leave me alone."

Miserably, I turn around and leave. Tears are running down my cheeks as I quietly shut the book behind me and I can hear Danielle crying. I hurry back to my room and curl up in my bed. After a few minutes I get up and go to the corner of my room. There are a whole pile of teddies there that add a cutesy look to the room. I pick up my worn pale purple teddy bear, the one I used to sleep with when I was little, and bring it back to bed with me, clinging onto it for comfort.

25

Danielle

I walk to school mechanically on Monday. I have my history and geography exams today, which I'm sure I'll fail. I haven't studied, plus I feel kind of sick. I hope I'm not coming down with that bug. On top of all that, I feel totally miserable. I am definitely in love with Mark and so is Rachel, plus Rachel's being so nice and understanding to me. If only she knew what I was thinking! I feel horrible. Plus Christmas Day is in six days and I will definitely not be able to enjoy it.

Naomi is back in, I discover. So is Liz.

"How was the disco?" Naomi wants to know.

"Alcohol-free," I inform her sweetly.

"And that's why you need me at those discos," she says triumphantly. "So, I hear Mark and Rachel were all over each other. Is it true?"

I nod miserably.

"What're you so upset about?" she asks me gently,

putting an arm around my shoulders and leading me into the corner of the classroom.

I remember how great Naomi was when my last boyfriend dumped me, and fill her in on the entire saga.

"Oh my God," is all she can manage to say.

"I know," I mutter miserably. I groan. "Ow, my stomach's killing me."

She makes a sympathetic face. "Is it that time of the month, or do you think you're coming down with that bug?"

"God, I hope not. I don't want to be sick over Christmas. Or getting my period, for that matter."

The bell rings for class and at that precise moment Mark walks in with a big grin on his face. I look down at my desk. It's covered with doodles and signatures and messages. One of them was put there by Naomi as a joke: Mark and Danielle surrounded by a heart. I look away from it.

***

It's hard pretending Mark doesn't exist, I realise. We're usually always messing around together between classes and it's hard avoiding him.

After our history exam, which I think I did well on – about a B – we have lunch. I search my school-bag for my laminated lunch pass and find it at the bottom of the bag. Caitlin, Naomi, Nicole and I walk out of the school together. Grace and Liz have opted to stay in school and study. Just as I think we're safe Mark, Robbie and Dónal join us.

I wonder which is worse – the mental anguish over Mark

and Rachel or the physical torture of my stomach doing somersaults. I decide they're co-conspiring against me to make my life a misery.

"Are you okay?" Naomi asks me. "You look so pale . . ."

Her voice sounds far away and distant. I can barely concentrate on it, I'm working on keeping my breakfast down. I feel awful. I just need to make it to my house, I tell myself.

It's not going to work. I can't make it. I lean over at the side of the road and throw up. I feel a strong pair of arms grabbing me as I teeter slightly. I feel really weak and helpless and scared, and suddenly I just burst into tears.

"Hey, it's okay," I can hear Mark murmuring, holding me close to him. "It's all right." He sort of propels me along the road. The others are following, I'm sure, but all I'm aware of is Mark. I can hear them asking me if I'm all right, and I manage to nod feebly.

We arrive at my house. I get my keys out of my pocket and try to open the door with them. They won't turn. Why won't they turn? Mark turns them for me and helps me inside.

"I'll stay with her for a while," Caitlin volunteers, and the rest of them leave.

I feel dizzy and nauseous and horribly sick.

"Caitlin . . . you can go if you want to," I say, even though I want her to stay.

"Come on, Danielle, you're not well. You've obviously got that horrible bug. Why don't you go to bed for a while? Naomi said you need to sleep it off."

"Okay," I agree weakly, and Caitlin and I go upstairs. She tells me she'll call around after school and I nod. Then I can hear her leaving, and I change into a long cotton nightdress and curl up in my bed.

***

When I wake up it's half past three and I feel better. The memory of getting sick comes back to me and my cheeks grow hot with embarrassment. Why did I have to get sick when Mark was around? I'm not sure I'll ever be able to face him again. Tomorrow we get our holidays. I really want to go in, to give my friends their presents. If I feel up to it I definitely will, I decide.

The doorbell rings. I pull on my dressinggown and go downstairs. I open the door. It's Mark. I'm suddenly aware of the fact I look absolutely awful, that my hair is a wreck, and that I'm wearing a dressinggown.

"Sorry . . . I thought you'd be up," he stammers.

"It's all right," I reassure him. "Rachel's not here, by the way. She'll be home in about ten minutes if you want to wait."

"Actually, I just wanted to see if you were okay."

"I feel all right now," I respond. "I'll probably be back in tomorrow." I gaze at his face. He's so gorgeous . . .

"Great. By the way, I found out you'll have to take the geography exam next term. They're holding repeats since so many people got that bug."

"Just what I need," I groan. I run my fingers through my hair. It's all tangled. "I look wrecked, don't I?"

"Nah. You look really pretty, actually."

I smile at him. Inside I feel there should be choirs of angels singing about that compliment.

"Thanks, Mark, don't know what I'd do without you." I sigh. "Well, see ya."

"See ya."

I love him, I think happily as I glide back upstairs. I love Mark so much.

26

Rachel

Danielle is in her night clothes when Mum and I arrive home.

"What's up with *you?*" I ask her.

"Got sick during lunch and stayed at home," she replies. "It's going around. I'm feeling better now, though, I'll go into school tomorrow. It's a half-day, anyway."

"What about your exams?" Mum wants to know.

Danielle shrugs. "I'll do the geography exam next term. Mark says they're going to have them again for anyone who missed the exams because of this stupid bug."

I go upstairs and into my room. It's dark already. It feels like about nine o' clock and it's really just after four. I switch on the light and change out of my uniform.

When I go downstairs, Caitlin and Naomi are there talking to Danielle in the sitting-room. Mum is hovering around looking disapproving that her sick little girl has her friends over, but she doesn't actually say anything.

"Hi," I greet them.

"Hi, Rachel," they reply.

"We just called over to leave Danielle's school-bag here," Caitlin explains, smiling. "Also to see if she'd be in tomorrow. Apparently she will be. I think Naomi's a bit disappointed. She was hoping to keep Danielle's present for herself!"

Naomi smiles sweetly. I'm a bit puzzled she doesn't start hitting Caitlin, but then I realise that Mum's eyes are on Naomi, watching her every move. I think Naomi knows she's disapproved of. Danielle looks totally embarrassed.

The doorbell rings again. I go out and get it. It's Nicole.

"Here to check on Danielle, huh?" I laugh as I open the door.

"Exactly. Has anyone else been here?"

"Caitlin and Naomi are in there." I lower my voice. "So's my mum, looking very disapproving. She thinks Naomi and you are a bad influence."

Nicole chuckles. "She won't after this," she promises. Mum comes out of the sitting room and Nicole turns on the charm.

"Hi, Mrs Connolly," she says very politely. "I'm Nicole Robinson, from Danielle's class at school. I just called around to see if she was all right. We were concerned about her in school. Is it okay if I see her?"

Mum looks stunned at this demure and innocent girl. "Of course," she stammers.

"Thanks. It was nice meeting you," she adds. Mum looks as if she's ready to collapse in shock as she goes into the kitchen. Once in the sitting room, Nicole and I explode in laughter.

"What's so funny?" Naomi wants to know.

"Nicole just put on the biggest *act* for Mum!" I choke out through my giggles.

"She looked absolutely shocked!" adds Nicole. "I guess I'm off the unsuitable-friend list, huh?"

"Definitely," I say, and we sink down onto the couch.

***

Once they've gone, I put on a video. A *Muppet Christmas Carol*. I feel in a Christmassy mood – not surprising, seeing as it's only another six days away. While the video is rewinding to the beginning, I drift into the living-room and gaze at our decorated Christmas tree. It already has some presents under it. I feel so happy and emotional. I always get like this at Christmas. I go back into the sitting room and curl up happily in an armchair and watch the film.

"Why is it," Danielle asks, entering the room, "that whenever Christmas comes around you turn into a total sap?"

I stick my tongue out at her. "I just love Christmas. The whole thing, not just shopping, unlike *some* people," I add pointedly. "And the discos."

At the mention of discos, Danielle's smile seems to fade away. "Don't mention discos," she mutters. "I don't think I ever want to go to another disco again."

"Why not?"

"Let's just say the last one didn't turn out as I hoped," she says softly.

I'm totally confused.

"Oh, well," she sighs, and then cheers up. "I suppose I should still go to the New Year's Eve disco though, right? I mean, to deprive those poor guys of me would just be cruel."

"Definitely," I laugh. "So tell me, what's the New Year's Eve disco like?"

"Great. The one for teenagers is on in my school, in the hall, because the adult one is in the community centre. It'll be deadly. All my friends will be there, unless they're still grounded. Last year, I remember, Mark and I had so much fun together . . . we must have danced every single song together . . ." She gets a dreamy look on her face.

I imagine Mark and me together at the disco this year and a big smile forms on my lips.

"Mum might not let you go, though," Danielle says sharply, interrupting my daydream.

"Why not?" I ask. "She let me go to the Christmas disco."

"Yeah, but that was just for first- and second-years. There'll be older teenagers at this one, and you know how Mum is."

"You went last year when you were only twelve," I protest.

"Yeah, but that's different. I was practically thirteen, and anyway Mum knows I can take care of myself. You'd be better off not going."

"I'm going," I say with determination. "I don't care, I'm going to that disco."

27

Danielle

While Rachel watches the rest of the film, I go in to Mum. She's cooking in the kitchen. I put on my best "Concerned Older Sister" act. Naomi would be proud.

"Rachel wants to go to the New Year's Eve disco," I say casually.

"Really? Well, she's a bit young, but as long as the two of you are there I don't think there'll be a problem."

"Well, as long as you're sure," I say, making sure it sounds like I think Mum's making a *big* mistake.

"Why wouldn't I be?"

I feel like screaming at her. She is not taking the hint.

"I just thought you'd be worried about Rachel being around older teenagers," I say, sounding hurt. "You know, like she might get into more trouble than she knows how to handle. But I'm being silly, I know."

Mum start to looks a bit worried. "Maybe you're right," she says thoughtfully. "I know you went at her age, but

124

you're used to discos and looking after yourself. Rachel isn't. I'd feel better if she waited a year or two before going."

"She'll be disappointed, but I'm sure she'll understand," I say, nodding and trying to look mature and wise. I hurry up to my room, a big grin on my face. With Rachel out of the way for this disco, it'll be just like old times for me and Mark. He might even forget about her completely! I turn on my Five CD and bounce around the room happily as I imagine how fantastic the New Year's Eve disco is going to be.

***

Mum brings up the subject of the disco that night. Rachel and I are leaning against the radiator to keep warm, despite Mum telling us not to, and *The Simpsons* are on TV. I'm half-watching and half-daydreaming.

The disco is going to be great, I think. It'll make up for the disappointing Christmas one. The Christmas one is usually the big one, the fun one, but this year we'll make the New Year's Eve disco one to remember. I'll wear the top I got from Miss Selfridge, the silvery glittery clingy one, with my jeans. Casual but stunning. I'll tell Mark that unfortunately Rachel wasn't able to come, and then we'll start dancing and messing around, as always, except this time it will mean much more to me because I love him so much.

"I hope you're not thinking of going to the New Year's Eve disco, are you?" Mum addresses Rachel.

Rachel looks up, surprised, and I innocently gaze at the TV. "Actually, I was," she says in a quiet but decisive tone.

"Now, Rachel, I think you're a bit young for it. Why don't you give it a miss this year, hmm?"

"I don't want to give it a miss." Her voice is calm and controlled. "I want to go the disco. Danielle and her friends are all going so I'll know lots of people there."

"Rachel, Danielle and her friends are nearly two years older than you. They're used to going to discos. You're not. I just don't want you getting into trouble, that's all."

"Mum! What kind of trouble, exactly, do you think I'm going to get into?" She sounds extremely annoyed. "Don't you trust me?"

"Of course I trust you, I just don't trust all the other older kids who will be at that disco. Do you understand? I'd prefer if you waited a year or two before going to those sorts of discos."

"But Mum!" Rachel protests.

"And that's final," Mum says sternly.

"I hate you!" Rachel screams suddenly at her and races upstairs. I hear her bedroom door slamming shut. I almost feel guilty, making her so upset, but then I push it away. I'm going to enjoy myself at this disco. She's already ruined one for me and I don't intend to let her destroy another.

28

Rachel

I sob into my pillow for what seems like an eternity. In a way, crying is sort of comforting.

I'm absolutely miserable. I hate my mum. I hate her so much. She's horrible. I want to go to the New Year's Eve disco. I want to dance with Mark again. I want to be cool Rachel again, instead of being nerdy Rachel, the brain who spends all her time studying.

I pick up one of my shoes and fling it against the wall. Then I take another and do the same. I can hear Mum screaming up at me from downstairs. I don't care. I turn on the radio and turn up the volume until I can't hear Mum any more. I lock the door to my bedroom so that she can't come in and give out to me. Feeling slightly satisfied, I stretch out on the bed and read.

***

Later that night, at about ten o' clock, Danielle comes into my room. "So you can't go to the disco, huh?"

"Well, *obviously*," I snap at her.

"I don't know where she got all those ideas from," Danielle comments. "I mean, I just said that the two of us were going to have a great time at the New Year's Eve disco, and then I made a joke about meeting older fellas. Do you think that might be the reason she's not letting you go?" Danielle looks upset. "God, I hope not. I was only kidding."

I can't get annoyed with her, she looks like she's on the verge of tears. "It doesn't really matter," I force myself to say. "Just do me a favour and keep an eye on Mark."

"Will do," she nods. "You know, I didn't want to mention this before, but Mark isn't exactly known for staying with the one girl for too long."

"Why not?"

"I suppose he just gets bored. You know, the way boys do. Oh, well. I suppose there's always a chance . . . well, I just thought I'd better tell you just so you'd be prepared if he did dump you. Just so you didn't get your hopes up, you know? It doesn't have anything to do with you. He's just not a one-girl type of guy."

I feel like crying. This must be my lowest point. Six days before Christmas Day, and I'm absolutely miserable. I can't go the disco and Mark is probably going to dump me. Of course he is. He probably thinks of me as the little sister type or something. My life is so depressing.

"Can you go now?" I choke out.

Danielle looks concerned. "Oh, God, I didn't mean to make you cry. Are you all right?" She hugs me. Her kindness only makes me feel worse. I burst into tears. She strokes my hair and murmurs comfortingly. I love my sister.

***

I feel awful the next morning. My eyes are sore from crying half the night and for the few hours I did manage to sleep, I must have been sleeping in an awkward position because the muscles in my shoulders and neck are aching.

I drag myself out of bed and have my All-Bran with ice-cold milk. Then, shivering the whole time, I pull on my school uniform. It's absolutely freezing. Even when I'm in my school uniform with my gabardine pulled tightly around me I'm still cold.

"Five more days to Christmas!" sings out Danielle, bouncing downstairs in her nightclothes as I get my school-bag and get ready to leave.

"See ya," I call to Danielle as Mum and I get into her car and she drops me off at the school. When I get into the classroom, there's frantic gift-exchanging going on. Siobhán, Julie and I give each other presents. I did intend to give Lauren something, but I guess I won't now.

I put mine in my school bag and firmly tell myself I won't open them until Christmas Day. Class begins with our teacher trotting into our classroom on her high heels and telling us that just because it's the last day of term and we're getting a half-day doesn't mean we can't get any work done.

Our second class is religion. Our religion teacher is basically very old and out of touch and easy to fool. We all hide in the locker room before class starts. We're in there giggling and chatting for about ten minutes before she finally comes in and tells us all to come on out now.

We have choir for our third class. Siobhán and I sit together and get given out to for talking twice. We don't get a black mark, though. The teachers are going easy on us today.

After break we're supposed to have maths, but the teacher is out so we go up to the supervision hall. Siobhán, Julie and I sit down together at the back and chat for a while but are told to quieten down. This gives me a chance to think about Mark. I replay practically every second of the Christmas disco in my mind, and I think of a couple of things I did and said that could have reminded him that I'm younger than him, and in his mind, not as mature.

I said "cool" way too often, I decide. He probably thought that was so immature. And maybe I wasn't that good at meeting him, I might have done something wrong without realising it.

I'm totally depressed when we go back to our classroom. I'm convinced I'll never see Mark again.

When noon comes, we all say bye to our friends and then leave. At least, I do. Mum is waiting for me in the car. I watch my friends hanging around for a while, chatting. I wish I went to the community school and didn't have to constantly rely on Mum for lifts. Also because I'd be in the same school as Mark . . .

You don't care about him, I tell myself firmly. And he doesn't like you, so just get over him! He's not important at all!

I just wish I could believe that.

29

Danielle

A group of us are hanging around outside the school after the bell goes. Naomi says she wants a cigarette. Nicole says, "Over my dead body."

"Come on, let's go over there for a minute and you can smoke," I suggest, pointing over to the steps that go up to the first-year classrooms.

Naomi reads between the lines and we sit down there. "What's up?" she asks.

"I'm just a horrible, manipulative bitch," I reply. I have my back to the others so that they can't see I'm about to cry.

"Well, I already knew that," she jokes. She lights a cigarette. "Seriously, though, what did you do?"

"Well, if we just go through how much of a bitch I was yesterday, that should only take about ten years," I say sarcastically. "Look, Naomi, you know the New Year's Eve disco? Rachel wanted to go and I secretly persuaded Mum she was too young. Then I went up to Rachel and completely lied, said I'd made some joke and could that have been why she wasn't allowed to go, and then I acted all upset so that she couldn't get angry with me."

Naomi bites her lip. "Ohhh . . ."

"That's not all," I continue gloomily. "I also managed to convince Rachel that Mark was this total flirt who never really stayed with one girl, and said he'd dump her soon, and *then* I did the supportive big-sister act. I am definitely the biggest cow in the entire world." I burst into tears. We get up from the steps and go around the corner, where the rest of the gang can't see us.

Naomi puts her arm around me. "It's not that bad," she says. "If Rachel doesn't go to that disco, it's not the end of the world. And if Mark really likes her, she'll realise he's not going to dump her, and if he does decide to dump her, you'll have prepared her."

"I guess so," I sniff.

"And," she continues, "if you spend all your time at the disco flirting and dancing with Mark, that's not exactly going to help the situation, is it?"

"You're psychic," I respond gloomily. She puts out her cigarette and I dry my eyes. Then we rejoin the group.

"Are you okay?" Caitlin asks. "You look like you've been crying."

"I'm fine," I say breezily. "Just fine."

***

Wednesday is the 21st of December. I spend it drifting aimlessly around the Square with Naomi and Jenny. I've bought my Christmas presents already. My friends and I are going to meet up in someone's house on Friday or Saturday and give each other presents. I can't wait. Christmas Day is on Sunday.

Naomi, Jenny and I go into McDonald's. Jenny buys a huge meal for herself. Naomi and I are practically broke so we share six nuggets, small fries, and buy a chocolate milkshake each.

We're slurping our milkshakes when a couple of girls from school show up. Liz is with them and they sit down at the table next to us. We're chatting for a while when one of them, Ciara, brings up the topic of Mark.

"I can't believe he met a girl two years younger than him!" Ciara exclaims. "I mean, he's *crazy* about her. But, like . . . she's so young!"

"That girl's Danielle's *sister*," Liz informs her.

"Oh." Ciara looks as if she wants to sink into the ground. Good. I smile slightly at her discomfort.

"Mark's such a babe, isn't he?" sighs one of the girls, Gillian.

"Mmm-hmm," Liz agrees.

Naomi sends me a sympathetic look. I smile at her.

"I always thought he fancied you, though," Ciara muses, looking at me. "I mean, the two of you are always flirting and at the discos you're always dancing and everything . . ."

"He needs someone he can be protective about," Jenny says. "That's why he gave up on Danielle. *And* Naomi *and* Nicole. They're too aggressive for him."

I don't want to be aggressive, I think. I want Mark to put

133

his arms around me and never let go. Am I going crazy or what?

***

When I get home there's only Mum there.

"Where's Rachel?" I ask.

"She went out with that nice boy. Mark, I think his name is. Do you know him?"

"Yeah," I whisper.

"Well, he came around here and they went out together. She'll be back for dinner. Did you want her for something?"

"No, it doesn't matter," I reply quietly. "I'm just going up to my room now. Call me when dinner's ready." I walk up to my room and sit down on the bed.

Don't cry, don't cry, I tell myself. Be strong.

It's no use. I burst into tears and I wish Mark was there to comfort me. But he's not, I think sadly. He's with Rachel, and that makes me cry even harder.

30

Rachel

"Where're Dónal and Nicole?" Mark wants to know. "They said they'd come."

"Be glad they're not here, for the moment," advises Caitlin. "Neither of them will put up with your smoking."

Robbie, Caitlin, Mark and I are hanging around the community school. It's deserted except for us, and we're sitting on the cold stone steps. Mark and Robbie are smoking cigarettes. I didn't know Mark smoked. Caitlin has delivered half-hearted lectures to both of them and then gave up. Like Nicole, she hates people smoking, I've learned.

A small figure approaches the school in a heavy coat. As it gets closer we can see it's Naomi. "Hi!" she yells.

"Hi," we all greet her. She sits down beside us and helps herself to a cigarette from the opened packet on the step. Removing a lighter from her jacket pocket, she expertly lights it.

"Please tell me Nicole isn't going to come," she mutters.

"She is," I say sweetly.

"Just great," Naomi moans. "Oh, well, while we can still actually enjoy ourselves, anyone want some cider?" She opens her jacket to reveal two bottles tucked under her arms. She sets them on the steps. I'm a little worried at first, but then Caitlin has some and I figure it can't be that bad. Anyway, I've always thought that although smoking was out of the question, drinking was kind of okay.

I lift the bottle and bring it to my lips. Everyone else looks shocked. I drink some and then ask, "What?"

"Nothing," Naomi says. "Just we always kind of thought you were a real goody-goody."

"Yeah, well, you were wrong," I say, and to prove it gulp down more of the cider.

"Guess we were," Mark says, and leans over to kiss me.

***

It starts getting darker but I don't care. Naomi drags Mark away for a moment and even though their voices are lowered, I can still hear them talking.

"So, you really like Rachel then, huh?" Naomi asks him.

"Yeah," he says. "She's great."

I'm ecstatic.

"But what about Danielle?" Naomi wants to know.

"What about her?" he says. What about her indeed, I think.

"You fancied her for ages! Are you just going to forget about it?"

"Look," Mark says, and his voice gets really quiet so I

have to strain to hear, "Danielle made it pretty clear she's not interested, okay? And Rachel's really nice."

YES! I think to myself.

"But what if Danielle was interested in you?" persists Naomi. "Which one would you choose?"

"It's a stupid question," he says angrily and rejoins the group. Naomi follows. I try to look as if I haven't overheard every word.

Nicole and Dónal finally arrive. Dónal describes exactly how Mark and Robbie's lungs must look right now and Nicole threatens to kill them if they don't quit smoking. I quietly ask Caitlin why Dónal is totally against smoking and she tells me it's because his parents smoke a lot. It makes sense in a way, I think.

The cider's almost gone. Nicole offers to go back to her house to get some beer or something, and Caitlin goes with her.

Mark puts his arm around my shoulder and I lean against him. So this is what love is like, I think happily. Naomi starts talking to me and I look at her from my comfortable position and feel like I'm in heaven.

A few minutes later Caitlin and Nicole return.

"No beer, no lager, nothing," says Nicole in disgust. Her coat is folded over her arm, hiding a bottle. She leaves it on the ground. "I could only get a bottle of vodka. My parents'd notice if anything else was missing."

"That's fine," Naomi reassures her.

I think, this is so cool! Really. It's incredible. Is this what Danielle's life is like all the time? She's so lucky.

Mark gets the bottle and we have a mock-fight over it. He wins and drinks some, then I have some. I'm starting to feel great, really confident and cool. I pull Mark to me and we kiss for ages. The others cheer and when it ends he kisses me again.

***

Later I make my way home. Caitlin and I are clutching each other and singing loudly. The boys have already reached their houses and we're on our own. It's dark out, but there are lights in the houses and the streetlights have come on as well, so we're fine.

"See ya," Caitlin sings.

"See ya!" I call back and walk to my house. I can't walk properly. I'm off-balance. I ring the doorbell.

"Hi, Danielle," I sing out. She looks like she's been crying. "Have you been crying? Have you? What's wrong, Danielle, huh?" The words aren't coming out right.

"God, Rachel, you're totally pissed, aren't you?" she says in shock.

"No, I'm not. I can't be. We only had a couple of drinks."

"If Mum or Dad see you, you're dead. Come on, up to your room," she says. "At least they think you were at Caitlin's house and not out drinking." She propels me upstairs and tells me to go to sleep. "You can tell me all about it in the morning," she says, and I lie down without getting out of my clothes and suddenly I feel so tired . . .

***

Rachel

My head is aching when I wake up. I sit up and feel dizzy. What's wrong with me? Danielle comes in to my room with a cup of tea.

"I know it's supposed to be coffee for hangovers," she apologises, "but I know you hate it and you like tea, and anyway there's as much caffeine or whatever it is in tea."

Then I remember. "What'd Mum and Dad say last night?" I ask weakly, sipping the hot tea.

"I just told them you were back from Caitlin's house and you were really tired so you went straight to bed. They didn't suspect a thing. Naturally. I mean they'd hardly think their precious genius twelve-year-old daughter would be out getting drunk, would they?" She sounds angry. "So where were you?"

"At the school," I say. "With Mark. And Caitlin, Naomi, Nicole . . . uh . . . Dónal . . . Robbie."

"Naomi?" Danielle asks. "Naomi?"

"Yeah," I say. "Look, my head is killing me. Can we talk later?"

"Sure," she says. She seems like she's in a daze. She walks out of my room and down the hall.

31

Danielle

"You stupid cow!" I scream down the phone line to Naomi. Thankfully my parents aren't home.

"What?" Naomi says. She sounds pretty wrecked. It's understandable.

"You went out drinking with my sister and Mark!" I yell at her. "How could you?"

"Ohhh," she groans. "Look, there were a load of us there. Caitlin and Robbie and Nicole . . . how was I supposed to know your twelve-year-old sister was going to show up? And that she'd get as pissed as the rest of us?"

My anger begins to recede. "I suppose . . . so what were the two of them like?"

She knows instantly I mean Rachel and Mark. "Very together, you know, sitting together and holding hands and getting off and all that."

"Shit," I mutter. "Any chance he'll dump her?"

"He's mad about her," Naomi says bluntly.

"Okay," I whisper. I know I'm going to start crying.

"I'm coming over," Naomi says. "I'm coming to cheer you up. We'll stuff our faces and rent a video. Any objections?"

"No."

"Good. Remember, a woman without a man is like a fish without a bicycle."

"You've really gone crazy, Naomi."

"I know, I know."

***

Naomi comes over half an hour later, armed with a box of chocolates she got for Christmas and opened already, two cans of Coke, and a copy of *Romy and Michelle's High School Reunion.*

"Great," I mutter when I see the video she's chosen. "Power to the bimbos!"

"Are you saying that all blondes are bimbos?" Naomi asks.

"Exactly," I say. "I mean, there's you . . ."

Naomi hits me on the shoulder. "Bitch," she says, but she's only messing.

"Come on, let's go watch two blonde bimbos be dumb," I say and we go into the sitting-room.

"So what'd your parents do?" Naomi asks when the video's over.

"What?"

"When Rachel came home drunk. I didn't think she'd actually get so pissed but I guess I was wrong. Anyway, did they give out to her?"

"They never found out. I brought her straight up to bed and told them she was just tired."

"Oh my God."

"What is it?"

"You. I mean, I thought you were angry with Rachel. Why didn't you just get her into trouble?"

"I don't know. I guess . . . and *please* tell me if this sounds too sappy! . . . she's my sister. Does that make *any* sense?"

"Yeah," Naomi smiles and nods. "Yeah, it does."

***

On Friday the 23rd, the whole gang comes over to my house carrying plastic bags full of Christmas presents. I almost ask where Tara is, like I have loads of times since she left. It just feels weird without her here. We've been friends since primary school.

Nicole and Grace have, as usual, spent loads on presents and made the rest of us feel guilty. Liz has got us all cosmetics. Just like last year. Jenny always gets us vouchers for various shops.

I hand out my presents. I bought jewellery for everyone this year. Mostly silver, it's cheaper. Everyone is passing around presents at the same time and as there are seven of us each giving six presents it's pretty confusing. Eventually we end up with the right presents and I leave mine under our Christmas tree. I'm dying to open them but there's just something that feels wrong about opening presents before December 25th.

After loads of hugging and "thank you"s and "you

shouldn't have!"s, everyone goes home. I sigh and curl up in the armchair beside the Christmas tree. Christmas seems ages away, even further away than it did two weeks ago, for some reason. Only two more days to go, I think happily.

"Look what Mark gave me," breathes Rachel, entering the room. She is holding a small gift-wrapped box in her hands.

"When'd you see Mark?" I ask curiously.

"I was just over at Michelle's house. Her brother, Eric, is in your school, I think. Mark came over to see him and he had my Christmas present with him."

"Oh." At least she didn't go over to his house.

"Should I open it, do you think?"

"*I* don't know. Why're you asking me?"

"Sor-ry. I was just asking, for God's sake." She looks upset and leaves the present under the tree. "I don't really feel like opening this now," she adds pointedly.

She wants me to feel guilty. I do, but I push it deep down inside. It's not fair that she should get a present from Mark. She barely knows him, after all, really.

"What's this?" she asks, holding up a couple of gift-wrapped presents with "Rachel" written on the cards.

"Oh, Caitlin left one of those for you. And I think the other one is from Nicole." My friends would have to get her presents, I think. They love her. Everyone loves my brilliant and wonderful sister. But what about me? I think they don't care.

32

Rachel

Christmas Eve arrives and I wake up feeling excited. Only another day to go, I say to myself.

Danielle is watching TV in the living-room in the morning, and I join her.

"Did you open Mark's present?" she asks me.

"No," I reply, looking at the small present lying underneath the tree. I've already given him his present, I dropped it over at his house last night.

I look at all the presents stacked up there. I can't wait to open them. Thinking about it makes me feel all excited and Christmassy.

"I can't wait until tomorrow!" Danielle and I say at exactly the same time, and then look at each other in amazement before we burst out laughing.

We slide down onto the floor and begin examining the presents. I try to figure out what Nicole's present is. It's quite small, maybe jewellery.

"Don't ask me, I have no idea," Danielle says. "I know what Caitlin got you, though."

"Tell me!" I plead.

"No," Danielle smirks.

After checking every single present addressed to us, and unsuccessfully trying to see what they are, we get dressed. Danielle is wearing a gorgeous outfit from C&A and I'm in a short black skirt, tights, and a black and white top.

"Gorgeous outfit," we compliment each other at the exact same time and then laugh.

Mark comes over just before lunch. Danielle and I both go to the door.

"I can only stay for a second," he says. "Just have your present, Danielle." He hands her a gift-wrapped rectangular object.

For a minute I wonder why he's giving her a present. Then I remember. I keep on forgetting Mark and Danielle have been friends for so long, even though they're constantly talking about each other.

"Thanks," she whispers. She looks like she's about to cry.

"Are you okay?" Mark asks her gently.

Her face cheers up. "Yeah, I'm fine," she smiles. "I'm just going to put this under the tree. See ya." She goes into the living-room.

"I'd better go," he says. "Oh, yeah, one more thing. My parents are having a party, like they do every year, and it's usually pretty boring, but she always gets me to invite some of my friends, and we watch a video or something. Danielle'll tell you all about it. Anyway, if the two of you can come, it starts at around seven-thirty and ends around eleven. See ya there."

"Yeah, see you," I call after him as he walks down the road.

It's going to be great, I just know it. God, being in Danielle's crowd is great! Discos, parties, drinking, feeling cool all the time . . . I love it. I used to be so jealous of her, but now I'm not.

***

"I'll come and collect you at eleven," Mum calls after me and Danielle.

"Yeah, sure," we reply and hurry away. Mum has delivered about ten lectures on the dangers of smoking, drinking, taking drugs, and disreputable young men with only one thing on their minds. And as usual we've ignored them.

We're wearing the same outfits we've been wearing all day, seeing as they're pretty dressy, and Danielle looks absolutely gorgeous with a hint of make-up on her already beautiful face. I feel a slight twinge of jealousy, then put it aside with a toss of my long hair.

When we arrive, Mark's mum answers. Dressed in a gorgeous dress and extremely high heels, she smiles sweetly and leads us into what she describes as the study.

The only ones I recognise, apart from Mark, are Naomi and Dónal. Naomi is smoking and Dónal is delivering a huge lecture on how smoking damages your health.

"Save it for your girlfriend," Naomi says carelessly and breathes smoke into his face.

"Hey, Rachel," some of them greet me, and I recognise some of them from two years ago, in primary school.

"How's life in the snob school?" teases one of them. "Our school not good enough for you, huh?"

"I just wanted to be in a school without you!" I retort smoothly.

"Aaaw, that's mean," he protests.

"Tough!" I say, and sit down on the floor beside Mark.

"Hi, Rache," he greets me. "You look great."

"Thanks," I say breezily but inside I'm glowing.

"Hi, Mark," says Danielle brightly.

"Hi," he replies.

"So what video are we watching?" I ask him.

"You don't want to know," he groans. "My mum said that we couldn't have anything over-18s."

"It's going to be crap," one of the boys volunteer from in front of us.

"What'd you get?" I ask.

He lifts up the remote control and presses the play button. "*Jingle All The Way?*" he says tentatively.

"Oh," I say. "Oh, well, good thing we're at the back. We can be naughty."

He pretends to be shocked. "I'm corrupting your innocence, little Rachel, am I?"

"Innocent?" Danielle joins in the conversation. "Rachel? Oh, yeah, very innocent is our little Rachel."

"I don't remember asking *you* to speak," I say in an obnoxious tone. I'm only teasing her.

"Fuck you," she snaps and gets up. She tries to storm out

147

but it's impossible as she has to climb over all the sitting people. She slams the door behind her.

"Oh, shit," mutters Mark.

"God, I was only messing." I bite my lip. "I'll go talk to her."

"No, I'll go," he says, and goes out of the room.

33

Danielle

I lean against the wall of Mark's hall and think how stupid I am. Why did I have to go and make a fool of myself in front of all those people? Just because Rachel said that stupid bitchy thing. Okay, I know she was only joking, but it hurt. She doesn't realise how horrible she's making me feel by getting so close to Mark.

The door of the study opens. Great, it'll be Rachel coming to apologise or Naomi coming to see what's wrong.

It's not. It's Mark. "Hey, you okay?" he asks in that gentle tone he has. I love it. I love him. So much.

"Yeah," I nod. "Can we talk for a sec?"

"Sure," he says, and we sit down on his stairs, side by side.

"I know I've been acting really weird lately," I start off, "and I think it's just that Rachel is becoming really friendly with Nicole and Caitlin and everyone, and I guess I was kinda worried they'd like her more . . . and then *you* started

149

fancying her . . . well, it was just sort of weird, that's all."

"You sure that's all it was?" he asks. God, he's so great. Most boys would be looking down at the ground, half-listening to what you were saying, wishing it was over so they could grope you or something. But Mark's not like that.

"Yeah," I nod. I look at his face. He's absolutely gorgeous. He looks at me, and for a moment I think he's going to kiss me and I want him to so badly . . .

Then the moment is lost, and he gets up. I follow.

"Thanks for listening," I whisper as we go back inside. We sit down on either side of Rachel. She whispers to see am I okay. I nod.

"Hi everyone!" a loud voice greets us, as Nicole strides into the room.

"Yo, blondie!" Eric calls out to her.

Nicole looks as if she wants to murder him. "You want your internal organs thrown out the window?" she threatens before gracefully sitting down beside Dónal.

We get bored with the video after about ten minutes and switch off the TV. We decide to play Spin The Bottle instead. Mark locks the door so that his mum can't wander in and we form a lopsided circle on the floor.

Nicole goes first and gets Robbie. Thankfully Caitlin isn't here, otherwise she'd go mental. Robbie gets Rachel and I sit back and watch. For ages no one gets me so I can just relax. I decide that all the boys here are okay, so there's no chance of me getting a total loser.

"Danielle! Space cadet!" Naomi waves her hand in front of my face.

"Hmm?" I say distractedly. Everyone laughs and Mark moves towards me. The empty Coke bottle is pointing towards me. Oh my God.

Don't think, Danielle, just do it. I lean over and meet him. It goes on for ages and the whole group are whistling. I feel like I'm in heaven. We break apart and everyone claps.

Oh my God, Rachel! I look over at her and she's fine. "Keep your hands off my fella," she teases. Amazingly, she's not pissed off about me meeting her boyfriend. Thank God.

"Go, Danielle," Adam reminds me, and I spin the bottle. I get Dónal and with him it's only a brush on the lips, trying to avoid it as much as possible.

"My fella not good enough or something?" demands Nicole. She's kidding, though, I know she is.

When one of the girls goes out to the bathroom she forgets to lock the study door when she comes back and just as Nicole and Eric are meeting each other, Mark's mum comes in looking shocked, and tells them to stop that disgraceful behaviour at once. She gives out hell to Mark while we're all still here and when she goes he rolls his eyes.

"Stupid cow," he mutters. "Oh, well, it's eleven o' clock."

There are lots of "Happy Christmas!"s called out, and then we leave the house. Mum hasn't arrived yet, so Rachel and I wait inside with Mark, and Naomi who is waiting for her next-door neighbour, at the adult party, to leave. From the sounds of it, the adult party is still going strong.

Naomi and I go into the hall, partly to leave Mark and Rachel alone, mostly because we want to talk.

"I think Mark still likes you," she volunteers. "I mean, when you were meeting him . . . wow! He looked so happy!"

"He likes Rachel," I snap. "He's mad about her. I lost my chance with him, Naomi. I had to be too confident and assertive, didn't I? Why couldn't I have been feminine and delicate? He'd have liked me then."

"Yeah, well, you're being feminine and delicate now, and although it's sickening, I think he's starting to realise you're not all loud and party-girl-ish."

"Party-girl-ish? Okay, I'm pretty sure that's not a word."

"Does it matter? Look, Danielle, let him see your sensitive side, encourage Rachel to be really loud and everything, and hey! You'll be together forever."

"And what happened to not wrecking Rachel's life?" I want to know.

"Fuck her! You and Mark are perfect for each other. I've always said so. Anyway, what about your caring big-sister thing?"

"Blame it on teenage mood swings," I reply, and I go to check if my mum's there yet.

34

Rachel

We have an agreement in our family not to start opening our Christmas presents until eight o' clock. Normally I'm up way before then, but seeing as Mum didn't pick us up until eleven-thirty last night – she was yapping away to some distant cousin she only phones about once a year – I got to bed late and therefore woke up late.

I bounce downstairs at ten to eight instead of my usual Christmas Day six-thirty. Danielle is poised over a present, waiting to rip off the wrapping paper as soon as eight o' clock arrives.

Mum and Dad come downstairs a few minutes later and the opening begins. First I open Caitlin's present, a Forever Friends address book. It's adorable. Nicole's present to me is smiley-face earrings. I feel guilty about not getting her anything, but Danielle tells me not to worry, Nicole always spends far too much on presents anyway.

I open Mark's present to reveal a beautiful pair of silver

earrings, in a gorgeous Celtic design, all swirling. I love them. They must have cost so much! I feel like crying. They're so beautiful. I love him.

"Let's see," Danielle says and leans over. "Wow," she breathes. "They're gorgeous."

I nod soundlessly. I can't believe he gave me these. Danielle apparently can't either. She's biting her nails.

"Stop biting your nails," Mum reprimands her. She looks at my present. "Who gave you those, dear?"

"Mark," I inform her.

"Mark? Who's Mark?" Dad wants to know.

"Her boyfriend," says Danielle in a neutral tone.

"Rachel has a boyfriend?" Dad says incredulously.

"Yes, Dad," I reply wearily.

"I'll have to keep you away from those discos in future," he jokes.

I make a face at him and replace my gold studs with my new earrings.

Danielle opens her present from Mark. It's a silver chain with cube-shaped beads on it, spelling out LOVE.

"What a kidder," she chuckles, but she sounds sad in some way. I can't figure it out. What's wrong with her?

***

Once we've unwrapped all our presents, we all go off our separate ways. Mum goes into the kitchen, Dad starts watching an old film on TV and Danielle and I go up to our rooms with our presents. I feel disappointed that it's all over. I always do, at Christmas. It's really only one day out of three hundred and sixty-five, and yet such a big deal is made of it that you spend half the year looking forward to it.

"Three hundred and sixty-five days to go until next Christmas!" Danielle says cheerfully, entering my room. "Hi, Rachel." She flops down on the bed. "So, what'd you think of Mark's present? I just hope he bought them this time."

"What do you mean?" I ask anxiously.

"Forget what I said," she says quickly.

"Danielle, what is it?"

"Nothing. I mean, I'm sure he's stopped doing it by now . . ."

"Doing *what*?"

"Nothing much. Just nicking stuff from shops, that sort of thing."

"What?" I gasp. "I can't believe it."

"Don't worry about it, I don't *think* he nicked your present . . . I hope not." She leans over and hugs me. "Listen, Rachel, don't worry about it. I'm sure it's all in the past, all right?" She smiles and leaves the room. I'm left feeling totally confused and miserable.

The thought that Mark would shoplift is enough to make me feel faint. Okay, I've always known that he and the rest of Danielle's crowd are far from perfect. Hanging around on the steps of the deserted school drinking and smoking isn't exactly a wholesome activity, but somehow, in my opinion, that's closer to being acceptable. I wouldn't have joined in, otherwise. But shoplifting . . . I just can't believe Mark would do something like that.

I reach up and touch the earrings Mark gave me. Did he actually buy them or are they stolen? They probably cost loads. Would he spend loads of money on a girl he's only known for a few weeks? A girl two years younger than him? I don't think so.

Mum calls up to us, telling us to get dressed as we're going to Mass in half an hour. I get dressed in a dress from Marks and Spencer that I picked out two months ago. I thought it was lovely then. Now I don't. It's babyish and boring and dull, perfect for the old, boring, nerdy Rachel. But I'm not like that any more. At least, I hope not. But if Mark's really as unreliable as Danielle says, if he's putting on a big act for me, will I be able to still go out with him? I don't think I will, and if that happens I might as well kiss everything goodbye. Being part of Danielle's crowd, being cool, being confident.

Danielle glides downstairs in a fabulous outfit from Miss Selfridge. She looks gorgeous, as always. I look down at the floor and try to think about something else, anything else besides my beautiful sister and Mark and everything. Unfortunately I can't. The silver earrings are still dangling from my ears. I start to take them off, then catch a glimpse of me wearing them in the mirror. They're so beautiful. Maybe I should give Mark the benefit of the doubt, I think hopefully. Maybe I should wait until I see him again before I make any judgements.

35

Danielle

"You're so *tall*!" coos my aunt Laura. She is speaking to both myself and Rachel, as we enter her house with our parents. Mass is over, Christmas dinner is several hours away and we are visiting Dad's sister Laura. She lives just outside Leixlip with her husband – my uncle, and their three children – my cousins. Bonnie is nine and idolises me and Rachel. Sophie and Tom are twins and they're five.

"Why don't you two go up to Bonnie? She's in her room," suggests Laura. "She got some new CDs and she's mad about them."

Rachel and I nod and hurry up. Bonnie's very sweet and anyway, anything's better than listening to the adults waffling on about politics and current events and sport and gossip.

Bonnie hugs us when we come in. She's a bit like Rachel, more mature than her age, if you know what I mean. She and Rachel get along well together.

Rachel seems pretty quiet. I know exactly why. I don't know why I'm such a bitch, but it's just . . . I can't really explain it, but when I think about Mark I know I'll do anything to get him, even if it means making my little sister miserable in the process. It sort of scares me, actually.

Rachel and I are admiring Bonnie's new CDs. Genuinely admiring them, not just *oohing* and *aahing* for her benefit. She has good taste. Bonnie goes downstairs for a moment to get us some drinks and I turn to Rachel. "Are you okay?"

"Okay? No, Danielle, I am definitely *not* okay."

She looks like she's about to cry, an expression that has become painfully familiar to me, and I hate myself, truly and utterly hate myself at that moment. I consider telling her the truth, that I made all that bad stuff up, but then I remember her and Mark at the Christmas disco and it's just like in those trashy romance novels, I feel my heart is breaking. My eyes well up with tears.

"Danielle?" Now Rachel is the concerned one, only her concern is genuine. "What's wrong?"

I quickly come up with an excuse. "Sorry . . . it's just that I can't stand the thought of Mark making you miserable, using you like he did all those other girls. You're my sister, Rache . . . I'm not going to let him do that to you."

"Thanks," whispers Rachel.

Inside of me, a voice is screaming "Manipulative bitch!" over and over again, and it's absolutely right.

***

Danielle

After Laura's house, it's back home for dinner. Rachel and I hurry up to our rooms and I can hear the parents muttering that it's so hard to have teenage daughters these days, you never know what to expect, and it's only just beginning.

I don't feel guilty anymore. Really, when you think about it, Mark and I have been friends for ages, and although we've agreed millions of times it just wouldn't work between us, things would have changed. Rachel's only known him a couple of weeks. She has no right to barge into my life and steal my friends. Anyway, she's too young for us. And too much of a goody-goody. I remember the night she came home drunk and imagine how Mum would have reacted if she'd caught her.

I'm doing this for Rachel's benefit, I tell myself. Some day she'll thank me.

Now, if only I believed any of this crap myself, life would be perfect.

***

Rachel and I may not have a lot in common – or used not, anyway – but we are both fussy eaters. At our Christmas dinner, with the beautiful centrepiece on the table, and fizzy drinks that Mum usually refuses to get on the table, Mum and Dad have their huge Christmas dinners. Rachel and I have small amounts of baked potatoes, small portions of turkey and tons of ham. We refuse everything else.

"What will we do with you?" moans Mum at regular intervals after trying to persuade us to have "just a tiny bit" of stuffing.

"We could always stuff them and roast them for next year," suggests Dad jokingly.

"Very funny," I mutter. I eat as much of my miniscule dinner as possible and then go up to my room. I put on the Celine Dion Christmas CD, *These Are Special Times*, and I turn up the volume on my CD player. When I pause it for a moment and realise that in the next room, on her cassette/CD player, Rachel is playing the copy of the album I made for her.

Amazing, I think. These little coincidences are becoming too frequent for my comfort. Saying the same thing at the same time, playing the same CD at the same time . . .

"Falling in love with the same boy at the same time," I add in a whisper. Then I laughed at myself for whispering. Mills and Boons romance novels have nothing on my life.

Oh, if only Rachel liked another boy, any other boy. If only I hadn't set her up with Mark. If only I had realised I felt this way before I tried to get them together! If only I was pretty and smart and athletic, just like Rachel. If only Mark liked me.

"If only," I mutter. "That's not going to get you anywhere, is it? Shut up and do something about it!" And I will, I think to myself. New Year's Eve is only six days away and counting.

36

Rachel

The days drag by. Mark doesn't call. Why not? He's away, I tell myself, visiting relatives, just like we're doing, half the time. Our timing's bad, that's what it is. It has to be. Right?

New Year's Eve arrives surprisingly fast. By that I mean it only seems like a century away from Christmas Day, as opposed to a millennium.

Danielle saunters into my room in a fabulous outfit for the disco. Her friends are going to call for her and they're all going to head up to the school together.

I feel extremely depressed. When her friends arrive, Danielle is doing her hair. Doing what to her hair, I wonder. There's not much you can do with hair that short. I answer the door.

A chorus of "hi"s greet me. Everyone seems friendly except Naomi, for some reason. There's just something about her and the way she's looking at me that makes me feel awkward and geeky. I know I look totally wrecked. My hair's a mess and I'm in jeans and a boring top.

I open the door of the sitting-room for Danielle's friends and they file in, except Nicole.

"You okay?" she whispers.

I shake my head. "No." I feel like crying.

"What's up?"

"Mark." I blink back tears. She notices. We go up to my room and Nicole goes in to Danielle for a moment. "Tell the others I'll catch up with you later, at the disco," she says. "I just need to talk to Rachel for a sec." When she returns we sit down on my bed.

I can hear them all going off, and then Nicole looks over at me with an incredibly understanding expression on her face. "What is it?" she asks.

"Mark. I think he's just using me." I struggle to stay under control.

"Why? Mark's crazy about you, you know."

"Danielle's been telling me all about him, about how he used all his other girlfriends and how he'll probably dump me . . ." I burst into tears and she hugs me.

"Hey, it's okay," she says. She leans back and looks me straight in the eye. "Look, this is really hard for me," she begins, "because I'm friends with you and I'm friends with Danielle, and I'm not sure what I should say to you, but . . ." she trails off for a moment.

"What?" I sniff.

"Um . . . can you just tell me again about all this stuff Danielle said?"

"That Mark could never stay with one girl for long and that he just uses them and that he'd dump me and I'd be miserable and everything, and then she told me about the shoplifting and stuff."

Nicole leaps up with such force that it startles me. "Oh my God!" She paces the room. "Rache, Danielle has been filling you up with a load of crap! Mark is not like that! Okay, so he's not perfect, he has his faults . . . he's a bit of a flirt sometimes, admittedly, but not when he's going with someone! And he smokes, which I have a *major* problem with, but if you don't mind that we won't count it. He's never *nicked* anything from a shop. I mean, God, he counts out the penny sweets in the shop very carefully, just to make sure he doesn't put an extra one in. Come *on*, Rachel."

I don't think I can say anything, except maybe force out an "Oh my God."

"I can't believe Danielle told you all that!" she exclaims.

"I'm going to kill her," I say.

"If I were you, I definitely would," she nods. "Come on, tell your mum you're coming over to my house to watch *Sesame Street* or something, that should please her, and then we'll go to the disco."

***

When we arrive at the school Nicole tells me to wait outside one of the classrooms. She goes around through the main door, flashing her ticket, and then hurries around to open the window and let me through. Together we go to the main hall, where a mass of secondary school pupils are dancing. It's crowded. I scan the crowd for Mark and Danielle but it's impossible to see them.

37

Danielle

Mark and I are messing around together, showing off, slagging each other, for the first few songs. I glance around the hall to see if Nicole's arrived yet, as Dónal's been looking for her. I see a girl with incredibly long dark hair turning around to talk to someone near the entrance, so that I can only see the back of her head, and for a moment I panic, thinking it's Rachel. Then I laugh at myself for being so stupid. Rachel's at home under the careful observation of our parents.

A slow song comes on, and Mark and I automatically put our arms around each other, without thinking. Until Rachel came along we always danced the slow ones together, just for the fun of it. He hesitates for a second but then smiles at me and we begin dancing. It's terrific, doing this again. I gaze into his eyes. He looks into mine and we lean towards each other. When our lips are about to touch someone taps us both firmly on the shoulder and we both look up in horror.

Rachel glares at both of us, her arms folded. "Hey, remember me?" she snaps. She has to yell to be heard over the music.

"Rachel!" Mark gasps. "I – uh – you don't understand –"

"Oh, please credit me with *some* intelligence. I'm not stupid. I know what's going on. At least you were only nearly kissing my sister, that's all. At least you didn't do what Danielle did." She glares at me.

I feel weak. This can't be happening, oh God, this is not possible.

"What did she do?" asks Mark, shocked.

"Oh, just filled me up with a load of crap about how you had loads of girlfriends and used them and then dumped them, and how you shoplifted and everything . . . and how those earrings you gave me were probably stolen . . ."

Mark gasps. I seriously want to die.

"Luckily Nicole set me straight on that," Rachel continues. "So, Danielle, what I want to know is, why'd you do it?"

I'm too stunned to answer.

"Well?" she asks. "Why'd you set me up with Mark and then tell me all those lies about him? Was it just some little sick game, to hurt me?"

"No," I whisper. "No. Rachel, I swear, I really did think you and Mark would be perfect for each other. Then I kind of realised that I wanted *me* and Mark to be perfect for each other."

I look at Rachel and Mark. They're both in shock.

"Because I love you," I whisper to Mark. Then the tears

begin to fall, until it's a cascade and I push my way out of there and into the girls' bathroom. There's a small, uncomfortable plastic bench which I sit on, and pull my knees up to my chest, where I cry like I've never cried before, great huge heaving sobs, making my body shake with misery.

Mark hates me, a voice inside me says, determined to keep me crying. Rachel hates me, Nicole must hate me now, and everyone will hate me when they find out about what I've done. Oh my God. It feels like my life's over.

"Hiya," says an unusually quietened-down Naomi, entering the bathroom. She sits down beside me. "It's not the end of the world, you know."

Grace comes in, looks around, sees us, and sits down. "Oh, Danielle, you poor thing," she says and hugs me. I feel absolutely pathetic, crying like a little girl into my friend's arms.

"It'll all blow over," says Naomi.

"Is everyone talking about it?" I sniff.

Naomi bites her lip. "Well, let's just say that everyone was watching you three with unveiled interest, practically drooling as they watched the dramatic scene unfold."

"I bet," I mutter.

"It's the most interesting thing that's happened in ages," Naomi says. "You should be proud."

Grace lets go of me and I look over at Naomi. "Are we back to being Naomi-the-bitch?" I want to know. "Because I was kind of hoping to get you in your supportive-friend mode."

"Sorry," she mutters.

"So what happened after I left?" I want to know, drying my eyes.

"Rachel went off into one of the classrooms crying and Mark went off to the boys' toilets, and everyone tried to pretend they hadn't been gawking," Naomi informs me.

"Big scene, huh?" I ask gloomily.

Grace nods. "Don't worry, though. They'll forget about it soon enough. Something more interesting will come along."

"Like the teachers doing The Full Monty?" I suggest sweetly.

Grace looks at Naomi. "Danielle's back to her old cheerful self," she mutters.

"Your life really should be a soap," Naomi says to me. "I can just picture it now."

"Yeah, just think," I groan.

"*Home and at School*," sings Grace to the tune of *Home and Away*.

"Not as catchy," Naomi advises.

"Could you two please get a life?" I tease them as we leave the bathroom.

"Oh, shut up," they chorus.

We stand around in the cold corridor. I'm not ready to go back into the disco yet, if ever.

38

Rachel

"My life can't get any worse," I sob. I'm sitting on one of the desks in a darkened classroom. Nicole and Caitlin are at either side of me, arms around me.

"It's going to be all right, Rache," soothes Caitlin.

"Okay, let's see," I say in false cheerfulness. "My sister set me up with Mark, told me a bunch of lies about him, now says she loves him, and he's going to choose her because he's mad about her. So I'm going to be miserable. Then, of course, I won't be able to hang around with you guys any more because of this whole thing, so I'll have no friends living near me, just my boring schoolfriends."

"Hey, you'll always be able to hang around with us," Nicole reassures me.

"Yeah," agrees Caitlin. "And you don't know for sure Mark'll choose Danielle."

"Oh, of course he will!" I practically spit out. "She's his age, for one thing, and she's popular and pretty and cool and athletic and basically everything I'm not!"

"Sounds like you're jealous of Danielle," observes Nicole.

"Why shouldn't I be?" I reply defensively.

"No, it's just that I've always got the impression *she* was jealous of *you*."

"What?" I say in amazement.

"You know, because you're so smart and pretty and everything."

"I'm not pretty," I object.

Caitlin snorts. "Rachel, you're absolutely gorgeous and if you don't know that you're crazy."

I dry my eyes. "You think so?"

Nicole groans. "You're just like Danielle. Both of you going around with gorgeous looks making the rest of us look awful and then you complain of not being pretty. It's sickening."

"Oh, shut up, Nicole. Look who's talking!" Caitlin laughs. She leans back and scrutinises Nicole and me. "The gorgeous blonde and the stunning brunette . . ." she says, sighing.

"We can't help it if we're beautiful," teases Nicole. She hops off the desk and drags me off as well. We pretend to be models on the catwalk. Caitlin boos. We stick out our tongues and then the three of us go out into the corridor and almost crash right into Danielle, Grace, and Naomi.

There's an awkward silence. I feel like crying all over again. The six of us stand there for a moment and then the silence is broken by Naomi. "How the hell did Jenny and Liz manage to escape this?" she wants to know. "We're standing around here with the tension rising and they're off dancing."

We all laugh. It's comfortable again, until the door of the boys' bathroom opens and Mark comes out. In the dark corridor it's hard to tell, but it looks like he's been crying. If he has I love him even more.

More silence. "Another mystery of the world," Naomi breaks the silence. "How come when girls are upset they cry their eyes out with their friends, but when boys are upset they won't let anyone near them?"

"It's in the genes," suggests Caitlin.

"Robbie's looking for you," Mark volunteers in a quiet voice.

"I'll go find him in a sec," Caitlin says. She's not going to miss one minute of this, I can tell.

Grace laughs. "Very subtle," she remarks.

"Hey, Mark, you all right?" Nicole asks him.

"No," he replies. He looks at me. I look down at the ground.

"I think . . . I think I'd better go home now," I say. I'm hoping Mark will say, "No, don't go!" and I'll know he still likes me.

"No, don't," Nicole says. "Phone your mum and tell her you won't be home for a while. Make up something. You have to stay until midnight, come on. "

"All right," I agree.

"Don't bother phoning, I'm going home," Danielle speaks up.

"Oh, why?" says Grace. "Come on, stay here."

"I'm not going back in there," Danielle says firmly. "They all hate me now. And I suppose all you guys do too, right?" She looks around. Everyone lowers their eyes. "I thought so. Well, since we've all agreed I'm the biggest bitch in the whole world, I'm going."

"Don't," Mark says.

"What?" she says.

"Don't go home."

I can feel a waterfall of tears ready to pour from my eyes but I try to look as though I'm fine. She got the "Don't go!" bit. I didn't. And once again, it is proven that Danielle is the nicer sister.

"Okay," she whispers.

A strangled sob escapes and I begin to cry.

"Rache . . ." Danielle says. She comes over to me and tries to comfort me. I fight her off.

"Rache, I'm sorry," Mark mutters, looking at the ground. He can't even bear to look at me, can he? I ignore him and turn on Danielle.

"Leave me alone, you bitch!" I scream at her. "I hate you!"

Danielle grabs me. "Rache, please," she begs. "Don't hate me."

"Why not? Give me one good reason!" I sob.

Now she begins to cry. "Because you're my sister," she chokes out. "And I know everyone else is going to hate me for the rest of my life but as long as you can forgive me it doesn't matter."

"Save it for someone who cares!" I yell at her and storm off, out of the school, into the cold, dark night.

39

Danielle

"She hates me," I sob. "My own sister hates me."

Mark pulls me to him and holds me. "She doesn't hate you," he reassures me. "She's just upset."

"Well, she has every reason to be," Nicole mutters.

"Leave it, Nicole," Naomi warns her.

"No, I won't leave it!" she protests. "I never thought you could be such a bitch, Danielle. Filling her up with a bunch of lies about Mark and then trying to steal her boyfriend at a disco that she wasn't allowed go to!" She glares at Mark. "And I can't believe you're willing to dump Rachel, who is absolutely wonderful, for this selfish cow!"

She storms off.

I feel so miserable right now. One of my best friends hates me. As for the rest of them, they probably do as well. My sister hates me. And it's all my fault, there's no one to blame but myself, I realise. Even having Mark's arms around me doesn't comfort me.

"What the hell's going on out here?" demands Eric. He is with Dónal, Jenny, Liz, Robbie and Adam, all curious to know what's up.

"Just a minor soap opera," mutters Grace. "Nothing major."

"Mark dumped Rachel for Danielle, that basically sums it up," says Caitlin. "Even though Danielle's been telling Rachel all these lies about Mark so that she'd stop going out with him and then Danielle could step in."

Once again I feel like I want to sink into the ground.

"You dumped Rachel?" demands Eric. He looks at Mark incredulously. "You dumped *Rachel*?"

"Wow, you're quick," mutters Robbie sarcastically.

"*Rachel*? I can't *believe* you, you *stupid* moron!" exclaims. Eric. "She's gorgeous and funny and smart and you dumped her?"

"And then she stormed out of the school," adds Caitlin sweetly.

Eric tries to casually slip away from the conversation and then runs down the corridor and out the main door. We laugh.

"So Danielle finally told you she's mad about you, huh?" Liz asks Mark.

"Well, all the girls are," he says jokingly. "Danielle just happens to be the greatest one."

"Finally!" Adam mutters. "We were wondering when you two would finally get together."

"Yes, but are they together?" Jenny asks. "I mean, they might decide – *again* – that it wouldn't work, and then it'd all be back where it started."

Amazing how no one else has anything better to talk about than me and Mark, isn't it? You'd think they had no lives of their own.

"What do you say, Danielle?" Mark asks me, gently wiping away my tears.

I smile at him and kiss him. I wish it could last forever. I'm aware of everyone clapping and whistling but it doesn't matter, somehow. All that matters is me and Mark.

When we break apart, we look at each other.

"We'd better go talk to Rachel," he says and I nod in agreement. "I feel really bad about this, you know," he adds.

Together we walk out of the school. Rachel is sitting on the steps, crying. Eric is beside her, his arm around her shoulder.

"Hey, Mark was stupid to dump you," he's saying. "If he doesn't appreciate you, you're better off without him."

"I guess so," Rachel says. Surprisingly, she sounds convinced.

"You need to find someone who'll be absolutely crazy about you, who'll think you're brilliant and wonderful and fantastic," he continues.

Mark and I exchange pleasantly surprised looks and turn around to go back in, and leave Eric and Rachel alone. Unfortunately they hear us.

"Oh, uh, um, hi, guys," Eric stammers, embarrassed.

"Hi," I smile. While Mark and Rachel look awkwardly at each other, I make kissy-faces at Eric. He blushes and makes a face at me.

"I'm really sorry, Rache," Mark says to her.

"These things happen," she says good-naturedly. "I'll live."

"Are you sure? I mean, I really did like you . . "

"It's just that you've always liked Danielle, I know, I know," she smiles.

For someone who's just been dumped, she's remarkably calm.

"And I really hope you don't hate me . . ." Mark continues.

"Of course I don't," she replies. She turns to me and says nothing, but her mouth is set in a hard line and her eyes are narrowed. "Go and dance with your boyfriend, Danielle," she says icily to me.

I have no option but to go back in and dance with Mark. In fact, I love it. The gossip is spreading like wildfire, of course, but I really don't care. I'm in Mark's arms and that's all that matters. At least, that's what I keep telling myself.

40

Rachel

"You didn't have to be so mean to her," Eric reprimands me.

"Why shouldn't I be?" I retort. "I mean, she'd make me miserable with all these lies and then act the supportive and caring sister! I'm not going to forgive her. Ever."

"But don't you think you might have done the same thing to her if it'd been you?" he asks.

"No way! I'd never be like that!"

"Suppose you wouldn't. You're too nice."

"Thanks," I reply quietly. I begin to blush.

"And shy," he observes.

"Sorry for living," I say. Then I shiver. "It's freezing out here," I complain. "Let's go back inside."

We stand up and go inside. When we reach the hall we push the heavy doors open and go in. A slow song is playing and I can see Danielle and Mark dancing together, both of them looking incredibly happy.

"Want to dance?" Eric asks me.

I nod and we move out into the centre of the hall. He puts his arms around me.

He's only dancing with you because he feels sorry for you, I tell myself. He's just a nice guy who's friendly to everyone. He doesn't really like you at all.

I smile at Nicole, who's dancing with Dónal and she smiles back. I spot Caitlin with Robbie and we exchange smiles.

When the song's over, we break apart, and my face is hot and red. I wonder what everyone thinks of me, dancing with Eric only minutes after Mark dumps me.

A fast song comes on and without thinking I begin moving to the music and singing along. After a while I realise that Eric's watching me and I blush, knowing he thinks I'm just an immature kid.

"What?" I mutter.

"I just didn't think you were such a good dancer, that's all," he replies.

"Thanks." I blush even more.

"I guess you're not used to compliments," he chuckles. "You go red every time I say something nice about you."

I don't have a clue how to respond to that, so I stay quiet.

"Oh well, by the time I'm finished commenting on everything good about you, you'll have got used to it," he grins. He begins to throw himself around the place. Actually, he's not that bad at dancing. I continue dancing and we're having a great time together.

***

By the end of the sixth song danced with Eric, I'm hot and flushed and need a drink. We go over and get Coke and gulp it down. I'm still roasting and we go out into the corridor, which is absolutely freezing, to cool off.

Naomi and Jenny come out of the girls' bathroom and have to walk past us. Jenny smiles tentatively at me. Naomi gives me a cool look and then glides by. I bite my lip.

"Naomi's pissed off with you," remarks Eric when they're inside the hall.

"She's one of Danielle's best friends. Of course she is," I reply.

"Well, Nicole's one of her best friends, too, and she took your side. In fact, she went off in a huff a little while ago. Lost her temper with Danielle, right after you went off, I think, and then she stormed off, back in the direction of the hall, I think. Practically knocked me down."

"Great," I groan. "I can't believe this is happening. I'm making everyone fight and get annoyed with each other. I'm never going to hang out with anyone here again if this is the way it's going to be."

"You can't do that," he protests. "Come on, you're exaggerating. It's not like it's the first time Nicole's lost it with Danielle, and Naomi gets huffy over every little thing anyway."

"Hmm," I say.

"And if you don't hang around with us, I won't get the chance to know you better," he continues. "And that would be awful."

"Really?" I ask.

He nods. "Of course, I'm not exactly in Mark's league, but some people actually do think I'm a nice guy."

"You are."

"Just nice?" He sounds disappointed.

"Very nice," I amend. "And sensitive. And considerate. And a good dancer."

"And good-looking?" he says hopefully.

"And vain," I tease him. "You're fishing for compliments, now."

"Hey, we're not all like you, everyone gushing over you all the time."

"Well, I must give the public something to look at," I joke.

He nods. "Always looking out for the little people, I see."

There's silence for a while. Then Caitlin and Robbie come out.

"Oh, hi," Caitlin greets us, and then drags Eric off for some unknown reason. Robbie and I exchange looks and then edge down towards them, listening carefully.

"Eric, what are you doing?" Caitlin asks. "Are you going to be the supportive friend who then turns into the boyfriend, because if I were you I'd watch it. Rachel isn't stupid."

"It's not like that," he defends himself. "Okay, so I kind of am helping her get over Mark, but not like that! We're just kind of joking around, you know?"

I start biting my nails. I don't want to be just joking around. I want him to like me.

"Okay," he continues, "so maybe I do fancy her, but that

doesn't mean I'm going to ask her to go with me! She's just broken up with Mark, for God's sake, and anyway, she doesn't fancy me. That all?" he demands.

Robbie and I surreptitiously edge back to our original spot and I find myself examining my nails, just to have something to do. Caitlin and Eric join us again and we begin gossiping about who's dancing with who. Eric and Robbie get bored quickly and begin a conversation about sports. Caitlin pulls me down the corridor with her until they can't hear us.

"What do you think of Eric?" she asks me.

"He's great, really." I'm not going to say too much.

"Great enough to slow-dance with?"

"Look, we're just having a bit of fun." I bite my lip. "Promise not to tell anyone?"

"Promise."

"Okay. I know this might sound like I'm a total slut or that I really never liked Mark, but I'm just finding that I really like Eric. As in *like* him, you know? God, I'm such a bitch, amn't I?"

"No, you're not," she reassures me. "Look, I think it's great that you're getting over Mark so quickly but don't rush into anything, okay?"

I nod. "I think I learnt my lesson last time," I mutter. Has it really only been a few weeks since the disco in the community centre where I first met Mark? It feels so much longer.

"Good luck with Eric," she whispers, and we join the boys and the four of us go into the hall.

41

Danielle

I wonder will anything be the same again. Probably not. Over the last few weeks, so much has happened, it's unbelievable.

Mark and I simultaneously look up at the clock high up on the wall. Eleven-thirty. Another half hour left of the year.

"My New Year's Resolution is going to be getting along with my sister," I decide.

"You going to go talk to her again?" Mark asks.

I nod. "Might as well get it over with this year," I say. I push my way through the crowd and find Rachel and Eric. They look awfully friendly for two people who've known each other for such a short time.

"Rache!" I call to her.

"What?" she snaps.

"Can we talk?" I ask.

"Fine," she says, and we go into the corridor again.

"I seem to be spending a lot of this disco out here," she mutters. "So what do you want to talk about?"

"I'm sorry for being so horrible, Rache."

"Good. You should be."

"I never meant to do it, I swear," I tell her. "I'm just crazy about him. Someday you'll understand."

"I already understand," she says tightly. "Danielle, I loved him too."

"I'm sorry . . ."

"But I just found out that there's someone who is way better for me than he is," she says with a grin.

My jaw literally drops. "Eric?" I gasp.

She nods. "I don't know what it is, but we get along so well," she says dreamily. "And he said that I shouldn't have been so mean to you."

"Great guy, that Eric is," I laugh when I hear the last part.

She laughs. "I suppose he's right. Anyway, I don't exactly see myself as the jealous, bitter type who ends up going crazy and stabbing both of you to death."

"So you forgive me?" I say hopefully.

"Yeah," she grins.

We hug.

"God, this evening is turning out to be pretty sappy," she comments.

"Not to mention a soap opera," I add.

"Or a talk show!" Rachel exclaims. "I can see it now, we'll tell Sally Jessy Raphael all about it."

"Oprah, I had a deprived childhood," I say, putting on a

serious look. "And then my formative teenage years were destroyed by my scheming younger sister . . ."

"More like you wrecked my life," she mutters.

"Did I?"

She smiles. "Oh, I can handle it. Especially with Eric around!"

I grin at her. "Come on, let's go back inside."

She goes over to Eric and I'm approached by Nicole. "Listen, sorry about earlier on," she says awkwardly. "I mean, you know the way I can get sometimes . . ."

"Mm-hmm," I smile. "It's fine. Really."

"Great. Listen, what's up with Eric and Rache?"

"Apparently she's already over Mark," I inform her.

"Quick work! But are you sure it's not a bit . . . rushed?"

"She's fancied Eric ever since she was eight. I guess Mark was just a distraction." I smile. "Which works out pretty well for me!"

She laughs. "See you, Danielle."

I catch Caitlin's eye as I squeeze through the crowd and we smile at each other, and I know we're still friends. I'm so happy . . . everything's going great.

I return to Mark. "I missed you," I grin.

"I am irresistible, amn't I?" he teases.

"Don't push your luck," I reply.

Rachel comes over to us. "Hi, guys," she greets us. "Hey, Mark, listen, um . . . the earrings . . ." She gestures to the earrings he gave her, which she's still wearing.

"What about them?" he asks while sliding his hand around me.

"Hand off my hip, Mark," I remind him sweetly.

"I wasn't doing anything!" he says innocently.

"Guys?" Rachel asks. "I'll only be a couple of minutes, you can do whatever you must do then . . . just please never tell me! Mark, listen, I think it would be really weird if I kept these . . ."

"Rache, they were a present, okay?"

"From when we were going together . . . it'd just feel wrong."

"Look, Rache, just think of them as being from a friend. And we are going to stay friends, right?"

"Sure, of course. Thanks. So, see you two . . . I've got to get back to Eric!" She grins and then hurries off.

***

A few minutes before midnight, the song "Perfect Year" is played. It's very appropriate, I think. As Mark and I hold on tightly to each other, I look around and see my friends with their boyfriends. Nicole and Dónal, Caitlin and Robbie. I see Rachel with Eric and smile at her. My sister – and one of my best friends – grins back. Then I think about Mark and how we're finally together . . . and how next year is going to be great.

And then the music stops and the countdown to midnight begins.

The End